Kissing Scars

Jim SHOMOS

Don't miss Jim's debut novel, Up Here

When you've had two dream marriages, choosing your eternal soulmate in heaven is one hell of a dilemma.

www.JimShomos.com/up-here

The most original romantic-comedy this century. Artisan Book Reviews, 5*

Up Here touched my soul, a beautiful romantic comedy about love, hope and courage. Alli, 5*

Jim Shomos must have written this with a twinkle in his eyes, as moving, as it is funny. Ella, 5*

Get VIP release news about Jim's coming books at:
www.JimShomos.com

Dedicated to

*Sunface, the woman who inspired this story and the character
'Sanaya'.*

This story is set in 2009/2010

PLATFORM ZERO

L eo gorged on the fruits of anticipation, sweet juices dribbling into his heart. Cruising into the city, 'Latika's Theme', the haunting romantic tune from the 'Slumdog Millionaire' soundtrack, played on repeat in his car. Each time the opening notes of the track restarted, his inner joy floated to another level.

The universe had been showering him with Indian themes. Born and bred in Melbourne, Leo hadn't been to India and had no plans to travel there. Yet recently, India kept strolling up, tapping on his shoulder, tugging on his sleeve, and Sanaya seemed destined to be his personal guide.

Stop projecting Leo, it's just a first date. But what a first date...

Not only did they both love the movie, Leo and Sanaya were actually going to replicate the romantic climax of Slumdog Millionaire, where Jamal and Latika were re-united at Victoria Station in Mumbai, except they were doing it at Melbourne's Flinders Street station. Even by his romantic standards, it was a gutsy first date. Sanaya's face could be the poster model for Indian beauty, innocence and joy, but he'd never have predicted her agreeing to his crazy idea.

Despite being a late-summer night, Melbourne's unpredictable climate tossed spears of cool air through the station's giant wind tunnels. He'd worn an embossed cotton white shirt with a sheer Indian style scarf draped around his neck; a colorful nod to the Indian inspiration of the night and a gesture for Mumbai-born Sanaya. Tonight's romance forecast: a warm evening under Sanaya's sunny smile, a touch of humidity in his heart and late showers of laughter as they settled into each other's orbit.

After the 8:00 p.m. scheduled meeting time, every train that slinked through, and every bundle of swaying dark hair in the distance, raised Leo's heart rate. He waited for his beautiful "Latika" to floodlight Platform 9 with her smile. Patience was not one of the traits that had been passed down from his humble Italian parents. Persistence: tick. Passion: tick. Patience: tick-tock, tick-tock, tick-tock...

By 8:45 p.m., Leo's shoulders were almost at hip level. Sanaya had not stepped off any carriage. She had not magically appeared on the wrong platform, revealed by a slow departing train. She did not float down the escalators behind him as a surprise. No response to his texts, no more music in his head and veins, no protection by his scarf from the internal windchill, which had dropped below zero.

Despite being forty-eight, the age where layers of cynicism and skepticism had forged thick anti-romantic walls in most of his friends, Leo was proud of remaining a hopeful romantic. But not as he was driving home at 9:42 p.m. that night.

I can't believe she didn't come.

Of all the first dates he'd ever arranged, he would never have picked Sanaya as the first woman to stand him up.

The only acceptable excuse: death or major illness to her, a close friend, or family.

It didn't help that he was listening to Love Song Dedications on Sun FM. The syrupy melodies and fairy tale lyrics deepened his melancholy of rejection. Some would call tuning in to this radio show just after being stood up as masochistic, but love songs were usually one of Leo's comfort foods. He could never remember the announcer's name but would recognize his voice anywhere. A voice which seamlessly drifted between celebrating a relationship, supporting someone's longing, or commiserating a break-up. A voice you wanted to hug. Leo had never been tempted to dedicate a song on this show. It was too easy and he took pride in his creative wooing. However, he secretly wondered if a woman might one day dedicate a song to him.

That would be nice. Forget it Leo, right now you don't even have a woman that wants to turn up on a first date.

The towering street lights and oncoming headlights seemed to be shining spotlights on his humiliation. He'd dumped his Indian scarf on the back floor, the sunset colors fought for space with Leo's feelings. He couldn't believe Sanaya stood him up on the most creative and romantic rendezvous he'd ever come up with. Sanaya had flowed with the idea, her enthusiasm bounced from her emailed commitment.

Honk! Honk!

The car horn blasted Leo back to the road. Lights flared his rear-vision mirror. Leo noticed the green traffic light and other cars already moving ahead. He eased forward and a big luxury SUV swung into the next lane with another blast from the horn as it zoomed past.

Death or major illness. No other excuse.

The next traffic light turned red and he stopped. He checked his rear-view mirror but no-one was behind him. No-one in the two lanes beside him. He flicked off the radio and scrolled down his phone music library. He needed a comfort song, a tune to take him far away from the night's disappointment. He chose the positive energy of the greatest love song ever written, hit play, turned up the volume, sat back and closed his eyes. The power of Angus Young's first chord on ACDC's 'You Shook Me All Night Long' transcended him out of his funk. It always did.

The light turned green and he accelerated onto the freeway.

He'd give her a chance. Tonight had been an audacious concept for a first date, a lot of extra pressure on a romantic ritual that was already a high anxiety initiation step. Maybe Sanaya panicked. Did he misjudge her? Wouldn't be the first time his heart had overreached. He'd give her a chance but he wouldn't chase her. He's all for the romance of pursuit, even though the word *stalker* gets bandied around too quickly these days. Being rejected for a date, or having a bad date, is an accepted pothole on Romantic Road. Standing someone up on a first date without any communication is way below ground zero in dating. Well below what he deserves.

He saw flashing blue and red police car lights on the side of the freeway ahead and slowed down. He laughed as he recognized the big black SUV that had honked him earlier. The police officer seemed to be writing up a fine. That bit of karma swung back quickly. Maybe it was a sign for more important things.

He'd give Sanaya a chance. One chance.

PLATFORM NINE

"I can't believe you really waited an hour at the station. You're a dag," said Sanaya with one of her favorite bits of Aussie slang. The way Aussies made fun of friends and kept them grounded with playful words, no malice, was one of her favorite bits of local culture.

"Do you think I write poems like that to everyone I meet? Plus, your confirmation was effusive." said Leo, his tenderness oozing out of her phone's speaker.

"I was being sarcastic."

Speaking inner-truth with her go-to goddess Lakshmi, she was bored with men's predictable attempts to get her attention, cheap high school lines always focused on her physical features. Leo's romanticism sprinkled Kashmiri chili powder in her veins. At twenty-eight, with seven years in Melbourne finding herself, Sanaya had fallen in love with the city but no one had made it through the front gate of her heart. She couldn't believe, not for one second, a guy would really want to meet her on the train platform like the beautiful moment in *Slumdog Millionaire*. That just didn't happen in real life.

"You on a train, in a tunnel? I think we lost signal," said Leo.

"You're just using train analogies to make me feel guilty."

"Guilt is wasted on anything that doesn't make your toes curl."

She exploded with laughter. Uncontrollable, nervous as a teenager laughter. Embarrassing, yet she didn't want it to stop. She uncurled her legs from the kitchen chair and leaned on her thighs to get some control…taking maybe an hour to rein it in. Embarrassing.

"Your laughter could pollinate flowers," said Leo.

She stopped breathing. Straightened up and pushed her chair back so he couldn't hear the pounding in her heart through the phone on the table. Forced herself to breathe. *It's just words Sanaya. Yes, it was the single most beautiful thing anyone has said to me. But just words.* Her mom's mantra crashed her inner-party, *"Words are petals, pretty but they fall away, shrivel and die. Love is the work that keeps your garden alive and love is action, every day, every choice in every moment."*

"I'm sorry about last night, Leo. I really am."

"I'll forgive you this time."

"Don't push it, dude. You either forgive or you don't."

"That's the second time this year forgiveness has been served to me with Indian spices."

She stopped twirling her hair, scratched at the

sudden itch burning her upper arm. "Indian women are your latest novelty thing?"

"No, no. *Shantaram* the book. The opening paragraphs have this powerful message about forgiveness. Have you read it?"

"No."

"*Shantaram* was inspired by the true story of a Melbourne man who'd escaped prison all the way to Mumbai and lived an almost unbelievable life between helping people in the slums by day and hustling with the Mumbai mafia at night."

"A book about a crook. Sounds like a subliminal warning."

Leo's uninhibited laughter bounced out of her phone, not one cynical molecule. By the time he settled, she could feel her smile from one elephant ear to the other.

"You're funny, can't wait for our first date," said Leo.

"You haven't forgiven me properly yet."

"Okay, I unconditionally forgive your cheeky soul."

"Hah! There's only one cheeky soul in this call."

"But I'm really out of cheekiness. I don't know how to top last night's attempt at a first date."

"You don't have to. Leave it to me."

"Okay, surprise me. Ciao, Sanaya,"

"Ciao, Leo."

She studied the three pictures featured on the lounge room wall. A classic studio portrait with her in the middle wearing a traditional sari; her mom on one side with a matching sari and long dark hair, her dad on the other side in a light blue suit and a shiny, bald head.

Another was with her cousin and friends, amongst a huge crowd, all of them drenched in colors during the Holi festival. She missed her cousin Ajala, the closest thing she had to a sabase dostie, but not as much as she expected. Being an only child had suited her; family and friends are fun in small doses.

The central photo featured Sanaya in a cap and gown at her graduation from Melbourne University for her psychology degree; she didn't like the way the cap pushed her ears out making them more elephant-like than they already were. Her parents beamed with pride. Which didn't last long after she told them she wouldn't be pursuing her Master's Degree in Psychology, that she'd chosen a degree in digital media at RMIT instead.

Distance is good. She loved her parents, no question. Yet, no matter how modern they were by Mumbai standards, their culture constrained them. Strained her relationship with them. She'd never felt relaxed talking to a guy over there; a million people could overhear any conversation and her mother seemed to know all of them.

The first time she witnessed Leo's intensity and humor, when he spoke at a digital media seminar, his passion physically filled the room. Sitting in the front row at a later seminar, his huge brown eyes sparkled with the energy of a twenty-one-year-old; they even made the grey flecks through his dark hair look more like fashion than aging. His romantic side since they connected threw a surprise. Sweet surprise or thinly veiled lure? She'd honor his crazy idea to meet at the station, but that's all. She'd treat the first date as research for an assignment, that's all. He was a handy contact for her Master's Degree in Digital Media and the career path percolating in the back of her mind.

Sanaya dived into her deleted emails and reread the four-line poem Leo had sent earlier that week:

Enough flirting with time
Let's set this train on the line
8:00 p.m. this Friday is where we'll find
Through the clocks on Platform 9

She felt so silly thinking it was just a poem. *How many guys on the planet think like this, let alone act like this? Maybe it is just an act? No he really did it. He waited an hour in the cold. For me.* Sitting at her barely four-seater wooden dining table, crammed into the corner of the apartment, she stared at the laptop screen. She clicked onto the first poem Leo sent her via Facebook a few weeks ago. He said it was inspired by her profile photo where she was holding a bright red apple to the camera; her "Twilight" moment with a feel-good spin.

APPLE SMILE
Tender bite from a ripe apple
Creates the sweetest smile
Fallen far from her tree
Tentative steps in a foreign garden
Suppressing a festival of emotions
Her seed needs a sensitive touch
The season for harvest celebrations
Just a moon or two away…

Sanaya let her eyes slow dance with the words for a few minutes then copied both poems onto a new page and saved it under a file she named "Leo Stuff". She scrunched up her legs into her chest, bare feet on the worn fabric seat, stretched her long red t-shirt over her creamy satin pj's and wrapped her arms around her shins. Her imagination swirled with words, flirted with lines. Her poetic ramblings usually meandered down lanes she hadn't planned or understood, she'd never written for a purpose, let alone a romantic path.

She un-scrunched her legs, leaned forward, and stared at the flashing cursor. All the words and lines scurried out of her brain. Just her and the passive-aggressive cursor. *The Cursor Curse could be a title. Stupid. As romantic as a Stephen King novel. Stupid.*

She pushed back her chair, picked up the empty mug and walked away. Later, she'd either be inspired or just write in simple English. Writing poems for a purpose isn't her thing. It isn't poetry and who was she kidding anyway? She's no poet. In her tiny kitchen the words flooded back in. She dropped the cup in the sink and ran to her laptop and brought it to the couch. Words seemed to dive straight from her head onto the page; her fingers barely keeping up.

She stared at the finished poem within the email. She'd typed it. On her laptop. But she didn't recognize it. Nothing like the usual esoteric nonsense scattered around her journal. She hit send and shut her computer.

Too bad if he doesn't like it.

MUMBAI TO MELBOURNE

Leo flicked from the email on his phone to his camera app and flipped it to selfie mode. He wanted to send Sanaya a pic of himself smiling in reaction to her email, but smiling while chewing on toast and marmalade made him look like the Joker in Batman. It would've made his twelve-year-old laugh and two teenage sons cringe. Luckily, they were with their mom this weekend. He put the phone on the table and scoffed down the last bit of toast, then pushed aside the remnants of his favorite Sunday brunch – scrambled eggs with smoked salmon, asparagus spears on the side, sourdough-rye toast, Grinders coffee, all finished off with the Warrandyte farmers' market marmalade.

Sanaya's poem deserved a larger screen. Tummy full, his heart filling, he pulled his laptop across the oval dining table and fired it up. With every line he digested, another burst of adrenaline and endorphins flooded his core structure. By the time he zoomed through the poem twice, he felt like he had no bones or creaky joints weighing him down. No gravity battling his body at all. He leaned back in the chair and adjusted the screen angle to read it again. This time in the slower rhythm her writing deserved.

'Platform 9 – Station of Clocks'
From Victoria Station
To Victoria's biggest station
Changing the day and time
But now we're on the same line.
Forgetting the rules
Courageous or two fools
What secrets will we unlock?
Walking through the station of clocks?
A Slumdog movie becomes real
Wear something with an Indian feel
Latika and Jamal led the way
See you in twenty-eight days.
No modern tools to call or text
Let mystery unfold what happens next
We don't need to look for a sign
If you're game to wait again on Platform 9.

Wow.

Leo knew Sanaya was special but this spun her onto a rare pedestal. The first woman who had written a poem for him. He was always attracted to women that could make him laugh, where the burden for fun wasn't always on his shoulders. But he never expected the same level of creative romance. He was happy giving without any expectation of return. *She wrote a poem... and in response to mine!*

Leo's eyes drifted from the screen, beyond the ash timber table and through the double glass sliding doors. The fruit trees in his yard and his neighbor's large gum tree swayed in the north wind. Melbourne's attention-seeking climate was already on the way to a scorching forty degrees outside. The room was cool thanks to the air conditioner, but inside Leo, the temperature was just how he liked it; sizzling with romance.

❧ 4 ❧

7 CROCS TO 1 SMILE

Sanaya first spun into Leo's orbit at a games seminar where he was one of the three speakers on a panel. Even from the back row of the packed room, her lustrous face - framed with a multi-colored scarf and long black hair – captivated him. After he'd caught her smile at one of his average jokes, he focused on Sanaya every time he stretched for humor. There may have been 150 paying attendees, but only one 150-kilowatt smile.

He never got to meet her as she disappeared before he could escape the obligatory rush from emerging games designers and a few digital media academics. This was part of the 'fee' he had to pay in exchange for his fifteen minutes of fame, having co-created Australia's first iPhone game that had broken out with a bit of global success.

Success being a very relative term. In the ten years since Leo had walked away from a lucrative sports marketing career, he'd never earned a half of his old salary in a year, cash-flowing his larger creative dreams with freelance copywriting for magazine, radio and online ads. After paying for his kids' private school fees and other support, he often had more month than money. Being broke in your forties wasn't fun, but it was for his kids and his dreams and you can't beat that for a double mission.

Leo muddled through like an imposter at these seminars. He wasn't technical or an academic. And the biggest crime of all, he wasn't even a gamer. He wanted to write humorous, clever pieces for magazines. Maybe one day write a book. Frustrated with his inability to get any creative work published, he turned up at a digital media seminar a year earlier. New online magazines and self-publishing opportunities intrigued him. The technology and process behind all of it scared him.

He'd almost drowned with boredom from all the digital terms and acronyms. But one speaker connected in non-tech English and inspired an idea for a game. Through most of the other seminar geeky gobbledygook, he feverishly scribbled out his idea. While at the networking lunch, he met Jason.

Jason lived for games and devoured technology, washing it down with gallons of Coke. At twenty-five, he and his first cousin-come-business-partner, Nicholas, had already built up a successful niche animation and digital technology company, "Pirate Bunnies". Introverted and totally non-business savvy, Jason and Nicholas stumbled into success after releasing a bunch of clever YouTube animations they made for fun. One ad agency saw their potential and they enjoyed steady lucrative work ever since.

Leo joined creative swords with Pirate Bunnies and three months later they released his concept, 7-Crocs. A silly game with seven different jungle locations; 'levels' in game-speak. To successfully achieve each level you had to navigate increasingly bizarre crocodiles. Being so early in the evolution of the iPhone, it wasn't hard to break through as an Australian 'first'. The international success was a bonus.

For the hyper superstitious Japanese, "7" is THE lucky number. Leo became aware of the fast take-up of iPhones in Japan, so at the last minute he convinced his partners to increase the number of levels from five to seven and rename the game. It worked. Japanese sales drove the game's ranking and helped sales around the early global iPhone adopters.

They became the darlings of Victoria's Digital Media Fund and won awards. But Jason and Nicholas didn't enjoy the pressure and hated the spotlight. They ditched the partnership with Leo and 7-Crocs and sailed back to their Pirate Bunnies cave where the ad agencies created the concepts and gave them cash just to make stuff. Leo earned enough money from the fad game to repay debts and avoid chasing freelance copywriting work. He rode the perception of success and enjoyed his new profile as a digital media guru.

His ego was in full shine during a Victoria Digital seminar, six months after he first spotted Sanaya. She'd attended another seminar in between but had sat at the back and disappeared before the end again. This time he was doing his thing as the headline presenter and Sanaya was in the front row. He took the speaking engagements seriously, keen to be transparent and give whatever value he could to the attendees. He needed all his professionalism to not focus on the siren a couple of yards from the stage.

At the end of his presentation, Sanaya hovered on her own at the back glass wall, enjoying the view of the Yarra River and gardens on the other side. This time he wasn't going to let her slip away and headed across the room as soon as he'd finished.

"Soaking in some nature to wash off the grimy digital talk?" said Leo.

He caught his breath as Sanaya faced him. It wasn't just her smile, or her unique beauty, the joy in her black eyes stilled him.

"That river always looks kinda grimy to me," she said.

He laughed. She beamed.

"You did okay up there," said Sanaya.

"Thanks, I had extra motivation."

Sanaya turned back to the river, but her lips shaped that smile again.

"Are you involved in games design?" asked Leo.

"Not yet. But I've got some ideas".

"Cool, when you're ready to do something, let me know…and I'll introduce you to someone that really knows games".

She looked up straight into his eyes.

"Yeah, my ideas will probably be over your head," she said grinning.

"May I have the honor of knowing the name of this future world-leading games guru?"

"Sanaya."

"Sanaya, that's a beautiful name."

"Thanks."

Sanaya's eyes took refuge in the Yarra view again.

"Are you originally from India?"

"Originally and forever."

Sparky. Fun. Fascinating.

"I have to catch a tram," she said as she picked up her leather knapsack.

"Let me give you a lift."

"You don't know where I live," Sanaya headed towards the door, "and that's the way it's staying," she said over her shoulder.

He followed her to the door. "May I have your number at least, so we can talk more?"

Sanaya hesitated, her eyes did return trips between the Yarra and Leo. Eventually she pulled out a pen and small notepad, scribbled something, then tore out the page and handed it to him.

"Facebook me. See ya." Sanaya spun then floated off.

"Ciao, ciao."

The piece of paper showed her full name, Sanaya Gupta. He watched her disappear amongst the afternoon tourists along the Yarra. It had taken all of Leo's willpower to not comment on how rare it was to see someone as beautiful as her anywhere, let alone at a digital media seminar. She'd been to three of his seminars in six months. Was that a coincidence? She seemed to be a legitimate gamer, but was she only there for the content? She'd worked her way from the back to a front row seat. Was his heart running preview screenings of a love story that didn't exist?

Sanaya had so much energy when she'd escaped Leo, she skipped the tram and ended up walking all the way home. It was a beautiful walk to Hawthorn, mostly along the Yarra River path. Walking was meditative, with or without music, her soul loved the serenity of walking. Except this time, Leo moments kept barging in; his silly jokes on stage, many she'd heard at the other two sessions, and the honest industry insights that were worth the entry fee. The cheeky rhythm of their banter. Close up, his eyes unraveled her; layers of sparkle and hints of endless fun, like a Diwali festival lit up at night.

Maybe not unravel, although it's good to call it, then she can just slot him into the file in her brain titled 'Boys, Beware'. Although Leo's not a boy. The energy and cheek of a boy, sure, but something else. Maybe just life experience. No more than that. Respectful edginess. Yes, he's respectful and she doesn't feel in danger, yet being around him spins the earth a little faster, on a different angle. Obviously, she'd get used to that and his true soul—or lack of—would slip through the cracks.

Halfway home, she sat down on the grassy embankment. A couple of seagulls edged close to her, hoping for easy food. She squirted them with her water bottle and they squawked away making her giggle.

Sanaya hadn't planned for that meeting to happen, to connect socially with Leo. Yet, something inside her suggested it was part of her plan all along.

Why did I attend three sessions where he was one of the speakers? Why sit front row at this one? I never sit front row. Third time lucky? Yes for him!

Sanaya laughed scattering the sneaky seagulls. She replaced her water bottle in her handbag and took out a notepad. When she flipped through the pages, she laughed again. Not one insight about game design and marketing. Lots of little drawings of Leo that she didn't realize she had created. Silly caricatures. Maybe she had gone overboard with the oversized head but those big eyes, they were oh-so real. She flipped the pages and laughed louder at her mini Leo cartoon.

5

MADVENTURE

L eo stared at the email on his laptop screen.

She wrote a poem. To me. For me.

Had any of his poems ever created the wonderful inner-warmth Sanaya's poem launched in him? He didn't care if an English teacher thought it was the worst arrangement of the alphabet they had ever seen. To Leo, this was amazing poetry. And a first.

But as he pulled up the calendar on his phone, the uncertainty of the date nagged him. Did 'encore after 28 days' mean twenty-eight days from his initial mix-up the other night, which would make the rendezvous February 7? Or twenty-eight days from the date she wrote her email, February 9? He didn't want another misunderstanding, which would be a catastrophe, so he fired off a text hoping for a quick response:

See you there in 28 days
Is what your poem says.
Unless you give a clearer sign,

Our smiles will dance on February nine…

Leo turned the call volume on his phone as high as it would go, placed it carefully on the table. Longing for a quick reply wasn't healthy. He thought about meditating again, but during a ten-minute session first thing that morning, Sanaya had kept breaking into his thoughts… he had no chance for inner peace now until Sanaya responded. He moved closer to the table and clicked through his laptop to the latest news on the Gunners. Scavenging online for stories about Arsenal was his go-to procrastination. Many of the UK football sites were the equivalent of trashy magazines and sometimes numbing the mind is the next best thing to stilling it.

Waste of time. Most of the stories are exactly that, mind-numbing fictional bits of rubbish aimed at addicted fans like him. He shut down the laptop.

Stared at the phone.

He leaned close to check the time; not even twenty minutes had passed since he'd sent the text.

Crazy Leo, you're not a teenager. Turn off the damn phone. Go and do something useful.

He stood and picked up the phone to turn it off when the text alert buzzed loudly, he almost dropped the phone. After juggling it to safety in his hand, he smiled at Sanaya's name on his screen then quickly clicked onto the message.

28 days from January ten,
Can you repeat your efforts then?
Follow the moon on Feb seven

Not six, nine or eleven
Could be our movie treasure
Let's not miss-time this madventure

Leo smiled. Another poem; plus she'd used one of his original words from their Facebook chats, 'madventure'. He clicked onto a website and checked where the moon would be on the 7th of February. He'd been entranced by the moon since he was a little boy, lying on the back lawn with his younger brother and sister at night as they made shapes out of the stars. His siblings saw shiny animals and cartoon characters, Leo only had eyes for the rabbit on the moon.

Sanaya had drawn Leo into a unique poetic zone, inspiring each other from verse to verse. His two-finger typing could barely keep up with the words flying around his head.

February seven can't come too soon,
What will we find under half a moon?
I'll be there within the time,
Wondering what our stars align.
Each train a tune of anticipation.
Dancing smiles across the station.
Can you schedule pure joy and pleasure?
I wouldn't miss this madventure…

Leo had arrived on Platform 9 at Flinders Street Station by 7:40 p.m. When he told his friend the next day he'd got there twenty minutes early, Paul knew that Sanaya must be special because Leo was rarely on time, let alone early.

He'd decided to follow exactly the same ritual as a month earlier. Smart blue jeans and white shirt with a linen feel. The textured pattern gave it a Grecian look. It worked well with the only thing he owned that had an 'Indian feel', the long Indian sunset scarf. He wore that over his neck, rather than wrapping it around, the brownish-red ends hanging around his knees, pointing to his tan boots. Despite being a balmy late-summer evening, the light scarf didn't bother him. Nothing could compete with his inner warmth anyway. Sanaya had an obvious wardrobe advantage with the theme and he couldn't help wondering what she would wear.

⁘

Sanaya stared out of the train window as the world flashed by. *Would Leo stand still, smiling as I approached? Would he be embarrassing and do some silly dance? If he dances, I'm turning around and catching the next train back.* The endless scenarios rolled through her mind with the same rhythm as the tracks beneath. Her tummy hosted a Ratha Saptami, the festival celebrating the Sun God. Which was kind of appropriate as Ratha Saptami was around this time of year back home.

As the train rolled into the darkness of the final underground section, her beaming smile reflected in the window. The harder she tried to clear her smile the brighter it became, until she burst out laughing. When she'd settled down a few passengers smirked her way, causing her to grin. She caressed the small leather handbag she'd bought in Hodka Village. Mostly crimson leather with stripes and intricate flower patterns, it was one of her favorite pieces of home—not exactly home as the village is in Gujarat, near the border with Pakistan and a long way from Mumbai—hand crafted by a tiny old man with a concentrated wrinkled face she would never forget.

Perfect for tonight's encounter with an old man.

She burst out laughing again and this time the grinners around her smiled.

❦

'Latika's Theme' was still oozing through Leo's ears after listening to it the entire thirty-minute drive into town. It added a sweet texture to the multi-layered soundtrack of a noisy Saturday night around Flinders Street station, Melbourne's major train hub, which externally looked very Indian.

Platform 9 was relatively quiet but the adjoining Platform 8 was filling with a horde of drunk tourists who had underestimated the Aussie sun that day. Their tomato-red faces added to the color of the balloons and ice-creams children were juggling with their parents. The tourists had peaked early, while local parents were zombied out in the young-family weary zone.

He'd taken up a position beside a steel green pole which rose and morphed into a gold painted support beam for the roof. Sanaya's rule was hard but added to the sweet tension; no communication for three weeks until they saw each other on the platform. He was so confident it would all work out, he'd turned his phone off before he'd left home. The electronic information sign hanging under the roof seemed to be talking just to him: *"2 min before Sanaya arrives".*

He tore his eyes away from the clock swearing he wouldn't check it again and stared beyond the tracks to Platform 10. Through the plane trees, the always busy Southgate bars and restaurants on the other side of the Yarra simmered. It never ceased to amaze him how much Melbourne had changed in the last twenty years. The city had proudly reclaimed the river from the ugly, old factories and rundown warehouses which had previously lined the banks and recreated this prime location for human interaction.

Squeaky metallic brakes of a train approaching Platform 9 made him yank his head back towards the tunnel on his left.

Must be Sanaya's.

His inner warmth swelled his stomach and lungs into a helium balloon. He estimated his position close to where the final carriage came to rest, near the escalators that floated people up to the main concourse. From here, he could watch everyone heading out and hopefully catch Sanaya approaching early. Saturday night revelers poured out of the silver doors. He studied the throng as they merged towards the escalators, tempted to stand on a bench.

Don't be stupid, she's coming here for our date, she won't disappear with the crowd. Surely she's just as keen and excited about finding me here as I am about her.

He glanced up the escalators just in case they'd missed each other; at around five-foot-two under her hair, it wasn't unreasonable. A piercing wolf-whistle made him spin back round. A group of tomato-faced tourists across the tracks laughed as one of them whistled again. He followed their gaze to Platform 9, but a bunch of tall teenagers bouncing a basketball between them dawdled towards him, blocking his view. They seemed to be the final passengers. Two cleaners rolled past in the other direction pushing trolleys of rags, mops, brooms and bins; one stopped and entered the final carriage next to him, the other squeezed between the lanky basketballers and the train. He hoped he wouldn't need the cleaners to sweep away another romantic catastrophe, dump his heart in a bin.

He moved aside for the basketballers and saw what the other guys were wolf-whistling at.

Sanaya. In a black skirt, silk orange-red blouse and solar smile.

A human sunrise.

His spine reached for the stars, veins bubbling with rocket fuel, heart almost launching through his ribs.

She swayed towards him; not a pronounced seasick inducing swagger like some higher-heeled women. Her open black shoes with low heel and leather laces wrapped elegantly above her ankle, suggested something more playful.

He ambled towards her, fighting the urge to rush. As Sanaya passed one of the lower lights, it spotlighted her long black hair naturally curling around her face; no overdose of shiny, sticky make-up. He loved that. From his experience a woman comfortable in her own skin was low-maintenance on an emotional level.

In that moment, just fifteen yards apart, he was a Zen moon to her solar smile.

Sanaya knew this train and platform well and had selected the front carriage because she guessed Leo would be waiting up the other end. She let the Saturday night party crowd scamper ahead of her. It gave her some time to compose as the internal Sun Dance festival throbbed with a thousand Indian drums in her tummy. She heard the wolf-whistles and laughter from the other track but ignored them; misogynistic rubbish was a step up from the racist litter she faced in her early Melbourne days.

She pulled down on her blouse and adjusted her skirt as the basketball dudes loped towards the escalators.

And there he was. Leo. Waiting at the end of the platform for the second time. Waiting for her. Leo's sparkly brown eyes a beacon that electrified and calmed her. They stopped less than a yard apart. The station lights flickered on above them as the sun disappeared behind the other end of the city.

He didn't hug her, or kiss cheeks, or touch at all. She had a foreign, unexpected urge to taste his lips but instead wrenched her eyes back to his. She was glad they had gone through with this ridiculous rendezvous and desperately hoped her own smile wasn't as gawky as the reflection she had glimpsed in the train window earlier.

She sensed a hint of vulnerability in Leo as he hesitated. Their imaginations and feelings had been so consumed by this first moment on Platform 9, maybe he wasn't sure how to start the rest of the date.

"I like your scarf," she said.

Leo slowly looked her up and down, then back to her eyes. "I like your everything."

"Looks like this is gonna be a short meeting," said Sanaya as she rolled her eyes.

"You are at least fifty percent responsible for this hyper romantic, borderline corny first meeting."

"Highly questionable movie-inspired moment. I don't do corny or romantic."

"Okay, no more corny compliments."

"Good, do you have something else planned or is that it?" She pointed up at the digital information clock hanging a little behind him. "My next train leaves in nine minutes."

Leo smiled then stretched his arm towards the escalators. "After you."

She stepped on and Leo joined one step behind her, to her right, making them eye level. As they glided up, she focused on the top of the escalators but felt the heat of his stare on the right side of her face.

6

OLD SCHOOL

Sanaya loved the way everything Leo said came out like a story with a beginning, a middle and end. Usually a funny end. She was captivated by Leo's brave journey from a well-paid day-job in sports marketing, into writing yet-to-be-published articles, which led to his abrupt tangent into games. It took a lot of courage to take a creative path when he also had to support three boys aged thirteen, fifteen and twenty. His divorce and children didn't blip on her emotional radar, it wasn't relevant to whatever their relationship might be. She couldn't picture Leo as a dad anyway, he was just an interesting guy who was obviously interested in her. And her interest was academic, not romantic.

I'm giggling too much. No more drinks.

They'd lucked onto corner stools near the edge of the rooftop Transit Cocktail Bar, perfect for the warm, autumn evening with a clear sky. Below, a few people watched an artist sketching outside Flinders Street station. Further to the left, across the bridge, the hyper busy Southbank area, and closer across the Yarra, stood the beautiful old boatsheds and gardens she enjoyed walking past.

"Enough about me. So, is your talent in the programming or creative side of games?" Leo asked.

"Guess."

Leo studied her a beat.

"Creative."

Sanaya nodded. "I understand coding but love the creative. Mom is a sculptor and art teacher. I started writing stories with my own drawings when I was in primary school."

"That's great you can do both. I couldn't draw to save my life and I'm allergic to any software, let alone coding. What does your dad do?"

"He's a senior toilet engineer." She braced herself for the usual jokes.

"Toilets?" Leo asked tentatively, "like public toilets, or home?"

Sanaya released her breath, stopped hiding behind her glass. She explained how her dad was the lead engineer in creating a revolutionary twin-pit design. It avoided the need for extensive piped sewage – which in India was a logistical and financial impossibility. The new toilets were transforming sanitary hygiene and safety in Indian villages.

"Safety?" asked Leo.

"Yeah, especially for women. They don't have to walk to a remote bush area, or wait till dark to... do their toilet thing in private. The indirect benefit of this system has been empowering for women."

"Wow, that's great, you must be really proud of him."

Sanaya nodded. *Okay, this guy is different. If it's an act, so far it's consistent.* She almost told him a more relevant secret, something that was bursting to come out, but Leo filled the gap.

"Even the rabbit's impressed," said Leo as he pointed to the third-quarter moon rising up from the east.

Sanaya soaked in their mutual attraction with the moon.

"Have you heard the story about how the rabbit got on the moon?" she said.

"No," said Leo excited, "I thought it was just a shape. Most people don't even see it."

"If you don't bore me too much, I might tell you the story some time."

"So there's going to be another time." If his tone wasn't teasing enough, the intensity and mischief in his eyes awakened parts of her body she'd ordered to stay home. Hopefully, her dark brown skin and venue lighting wouldn't give her away.

"I think your eyes are blushing."

CHEEEEEKY MONKEY.

She diverted her gaze to the pretty carriage dragged by two big draught horses across Princess Bridge; parents and two young children, about four or five in the carriage. The boy kept standing up and jumping playfully while his dad tried to calm him. Seemed like a hopeless cause and she wondered if Leo had the same endless energy as a kid.

"Let's take a ride later," said Leo.

"Nah. That's for tourists and people that think they're in love."

Maybe there was bit of an edge in that but I need to throw a boundary warning in.

He didn't blink. Grinned then pointed to her almost empty glass.

"Another daiquiri?"

She hesitated, pulled out her phone and checked the time. She'd already had two and it was just after ten. Her mantra for the night was, no matter how well the night went, she would leave by ten. If this was as good as it promised they'd have plenty of times to get to know each other. Her 'no rushing' policy flushed out the dudes focused only on flesh. Another little challenge for him. She drained the last dregs of her rum and strawberry cocktail then lowered the glass back to the table.

"Sure, why not?"

"My favorite three words."

Leo was halfway to the bar before she had a chance to think about how the words which spilled out of her mouth were the opposite of those swirling around her head. She might be tipsy but she wasn't drunk. She laughed. *Okay, curfew now is definitely eleven. No negotiation.* She set her phone alarm on and put it back in her bag. Then took it out again, turned it to vibrate and left the bag on her lap, rather than hanging over her chair. *He doesn't need to know I have a curfew alarm.* As she watched Leo work his way through the bar crowd, she noted for the first time that he hadn't pulled out his phone once tonight. There must have been dozens of other people focused on phones all around the bar. But not Leo. *Maybe he has no friends!* Her laughter exploded. Most of the guys she'd been around were constantly doing something on their phone; SMS or sport, or checking their precious non-social media. Leo wasn't just older, he was old-school. *That's cool.*

❧

Leo was disappointed Sanaya wanted to go home at 11:00 p.m. Conversation had flowed like chocolate sauce on a pudding, her laugh could've replaced all the lighting in the CBD; and she was funny. Proper… grounded…funny. She seemed ignorant of her beauty rather than her beauty feeding any kind of arrogance.

So beautiful. The way she floats her hands around when she talks…

He had managed to slow her down for a few minutes outside the station as they watched a street artist do pencil portraits for people. She took her time looking over all his work but it didn't seem long enough.

As he waved to her through the moving train window, she put on a serious face and mimicked Queen Elizabeth's royal wave. He began to copy her with his right hand then brought his thumb to his ear and flapped his hand. Leo was sure he could hear Sanaya's laugh despite the noisy train leaving Platform 9 as another squealed to a stop on Platform 8.

Floating home with 'Latika's Theme' on repeat again, Leo decided he should finally send that 'thank you' email he'd been intending for the Slumdog Millionaire composer, A.R. Rahman. Yes, and he would also send an email to the film's director Danny Boyle and writer Simon Beaufoy. And to Sanaya's toilet-engineer dad and her art-teacher mom. Something like: *Thank you all for your unknown collaboration in bringing Sanaya and me together. Whatever happens from here, I'm not wise enough to know. But I'm proud of us both being brave enough to launch our romantic rocket, fueled by your creative and romantic spirits...*

Maybe he'd just write to A.R. Rahman...

Sanaya's thoughts gently swayed with the train. She was proud of her 11:00 p.m. escape and the simple kiss-on-the-cheek goodbye. He was ever so gentle and she could still feel his warm lips on her skin. Her academic interest had evolved into a different kind of curiosity. Who was she trying to kid? It was always a date. In all honesty, secret not-to-tell-Leo honesty, that was her best first date ever. Not that she'd had that many dates. But it was way better than she had imagined.

No way would she share that with Leo. Give a guy like him a sweet apple and he'd want your whole fruit shop.

7

PHEROMONE COCKTAIL

Sanaya studied Leo through her eyebrows, her head bent down a little, wondering whether to slam another one of his corny lines.

"To courage in filmmaking and crazy first dates," Leo had toasted. His hot chocolate hovered between them.

She lifted her latte. "To courage," she said, and clinked his cup with her glass.

She was kind of chuffed he was still buzzing after seeing Slumdog Millionaire together at the Nova Cinema's re-release of the film post Oscars glory. Her suggestion was an obvious choice for their second date. Sanaya and Leo were sitting on stools at a window overlooking the trend-seeking tables outside Brunetti's. Sanaya loved this cake and coffee institution in Carlton. The mixture of old shops that had been merged together into one large hive. The endless rows of tempting sweets. The energy and conversations buzzing around.

"I'm so glad I saw it again. There's so much stuff happening on different levels, it's cool how it all comes together in the end," said Sanaya as she stirred her latte.

"They set it up like a caper movie. Did he cheat or didn't he? Is he cheating on his own or part of a syndicate? Will he get away with it? Then it turns into a buddy journey with his brother and young Latika. But in the end, it's an epic love story. Beautiful," said Leo.

They were sitting close, their bodies angled towards each other as they leaned on the high narrow bench table along the window. His left foot was resting on the low rung of her stool, his shin nestling into her right calf. She was struggling to focus with the energy zipping through her jeans, zapping electricity across her whole body. Leo seemed oblivious to it as he sipped his dark Italian hot chocolate, the kind that had no milk and if you put a spoon in the middle of the cup it would stand on its own.

"If I got cancer or something, just put me in a bath filled with this hot chocolate and let me drown," he said.

Was he always this passionate? This alive, even when speaking about death? It was hard not to get swept up in his enthusiasm, his child-like positivity. She'd had a moment of fear straight after the movie. Was she just Leo's token Indian? His fantasy Latika? But the way he stared at her. The way his eyes shone into her soul, surely that was real. She would have to take it slowly, all the mistakes she'd ever made came from rushing decisions. Slow is her trusted friend.

She had trammed in —trams were her first Melbourne love— and met Leo at the Nova, but when

Leo offered her a lift home that night she saw no reason to turn it down. She felt safe with him. Initially, she was surprised by his conservative mid-sized family car, but it was clean and relatively new. She guessed he had to have some practical side considering the three kids he needed to cart around. Besides, she didn't have a car at all, so who was she to judge.

It wasn't until they approached her apartment in Prahran that her nerves had started tingling. She wasn't sure exactly why. In her head, this was clearly just a lift. Nothing else was going to happen. She was sure about that.

I'm taking it slow. We're taking it slow. Slow is my friend.

Walking from his car together, Leo was sure they'd have their first kiss tonight. It wasn't just the easy banter and laughter through the night. At Brunetti's, his left leg often brushed up against Sanaya's right leg, sometimes for ages. He knew women don't let that happen unless they're comfortable with you, or flirting, or both. They'd definitely ramped up the most important measure in the development of any relationship tonight: enjoying more-laughs-per-minute. The casual touching was stage two. From here anything could happen.

"This is it," said Sanaya stopping, "I'm up there." She vaguely pointed to the second floor.

Her apartment building wasn't one of the new modern designs slowly taking over the inner-Melbourne suburbs. This was a stubborn, old block that liked where it was and had no plans to be bullied by the big, new kids in town. Just three stories high in a lane on the suburban east side of High Street. There was a long driveway between the carport on the street side and the building.

"I had a terrible time," Leo said, getting the jump on her blasé-ness.

"Finally, we're in synch," said Sanaya. "Lucky the movie was good."

Her instant retort made him smile. Even by her standards that was good. But they'd been in synch all night. Plus, Sanaya wasn't moving. She didn't wave, or say goodbye, or head to the entrance. He sensed her hesitation and stepped close.

༒

In a surreal third-person experience Sanaya could see herself walking towards the entrance of her building while her identical twin was standing at the top of the driveway, staring into Leo's eyes. In the dim street light, his pupils were huge, yet still surrounded by acres of lush brown. Leo slowly moved in to kiss her.

Like a dog chasing its tail, blood cells chased each other around her veins, her head, and her heart. She felt dizzy yet more centered and in the moment than she'd ever been, stretching her calves, moving her mouth towards his. His lips moist, pulsating energy through to her core. Her breath and tummy flinched as Leo's right hand breezed over her cheek, palm open. His fingers found a home in her hair, his thumb launched more raging blood as it caressed her ear lobe and neck.

After what seemed like an eternity, Leo pulled back. Fire in his earthy eyes.

She had discovered an aching she didn't know her body was capable of. A lava sparked by those rampaging blood cells and now mixed with endorphins, pheromones and adrenaline. The most delicious cocktail she had ever tasted.

Leo must have had a million first-kisses, but the way his eyes burned through hers, it seemed like he was drowning in the same cocktail. Sanaya's third-person twin was behind her now, nudging her closer, tighter into Leo. He kissed her again, this time sliding his arms around her lower back. She simultaneously shivered and wrapped her arms around his shoulders, hands following foreign instincts, exploring the heat through his shirt. Holding him felt familiar, new, exhilarating. His lips and tongue led hers through yoga-like contortions. Hot steamy Bikram yoga. No control. No fear. Only the heat and taste of Leo.

Eventually, she broke the spell, breaking away. They stood there, a few inches apart, breathing heavily.

"Wow," said Leo.

She was impressed he could find a single syllable. Her heart, lungs and brain couldn't collaborate on anything; like her first day in Melbourne, on ground she didn't know and feeling totally out of place. She slowly backed away from Leo toward the main door.

"Good night, Sanaya," whispered Leo.

It took a few more backward steps before she responded.

"Good night, Leo." It was a husky, barely audible voice. Like much of the last few minutes, Sanaya didn't recognize it. She turned and reached the door quickly, determined not to run, determined not to turn back.

8

INDIAN SUMMER

Sanaya was glad to be away most of the next ten days for her cousin's wedding in Mumbai. It gave her time to digest what had happened with Leo on safe, distant ground. It was fun catching up with Ajala and her other cousins, even her parents. A perfect excuse for minimal or no communication with Leo.

It wasn't easy.

Memories of his eyes and that kiss regularly stormed into her thoughts, demanding attention. She remained determined enough to not encourage any communication with him while she was away. Maybe she was over thinking the whole thing considering they'd only been on two dates. Despite Ajala's wedding having the traditional three days of events including the long, but beautiful ceremony around the fire, Sanaya's mom had slotted in three introductions to potential husbands for the last four days of her stay.

"I'm not going to a husband sale."

"They are most certainly not husband sales, Sanaya.

We are just meeting with family friends," said her mother.

"Who happen to all have a boring son still here and still single."

"They are engineers like your father, an accountant and one is studying to be a doctor. A doctor who likes you very much."

Her mother on her knees, guided Sanaya forty-five degrees to the left then adjusted the fabric on the top part of her lengha a touch lower.

"I haven't seen Doc Naji since high school, he'll die of diabetes before becoming a doctor."

"Melbourne has made you rude and shallow. You need to find someone with a good heart and soul."

And an amazing kiss. And a body that can survive sex without an ambulance on hold.

"You've got it wrong mom Melbourne hasn't made me, I've made Melbourne. After I moved there, it keeps winning The World's Most Livable City."

Mom did the head shake and eye glare thing that only Indian mothers can do. "We'll talk more with your father, after the wedding." She fixed one more pin on the dress then stood back. Love and pride oozed from her and melted Sanaya's defiance.

"You'll be the most sundar sssingle woman at the wedding."

Sundar for beautiful, stunning, graceful.

SSSingle for sad, shameful, failure.

She loved her parents and was proud of the history of her birth country but every trip home highlighted how much their generation gap was magnified by a cultural gap. Her parents were deeply in love after thirty years despite starting as strangers in an arranged marriage. A better example than fifty percent of western marriages which ended in divorce. Maybe better than seventy-five percent. She wasn't anti-marriage, or even anti-arranged marriage; just anti-mom-pushing-marriage. She also didn't believe in love-at-first-sight or the myth of romantic destiny. She had to be careful with Leo when she got back to Melbourne because he was either a top-class charmer or a walking ro-man-tic.

Both dangerous.

"Thanks, Mom." The top section was a touch lower, revealing less of her tummy than she'd planned but she needed to give her mom one win.

۞

Sanaya was overjoyed for Ajala during the wedding ceremony and enjoyed every little ritual. The mandap was a vibrant mix of fabric colors and flowers yet her eyes kept drifting to the little fire in the center on the floor. The flames took her back to Leo's eyes. The time they connected after his seminar, the night they met at Flinders Street station, before and after that first kiss. The passionate, planet-spinning first kiss.

"You should sit back further from the fire, your cheeks are red," said her mother, the only person who could tell the subtle shifts in her skin.

By the time Ajala and her shiny husband had completed the traditional seven laps of the fire, Sanaya had made a decision. She'd book a flight back for the next day. Before her mother's arranged 'family gatherings'.

Leo had squeezed into a seat on her life train like he'd been there from the beginning of her adult journey.

Haasyaaspad.

Ridiculous.

The only way to prove how haasyaapad was to lob Leo with the non-negotiable life-grenade that made it clear they had no long-term destiny.

❧

Leo struggled with Sanaya's trip. Despite meditation and major love lessons in recent years, he couldn't stop falling hard and fast for Sanaya. A couple of his not-so-romantic friends had called him intense; how sad they didn't have the courage to follow their hearts. Each relationship flows and grows on its own momentum. Some you need to paddle hard in a static lagoon. Others drift on a serene stream for ages before merging into a romantic river. Sanaya dragged him into an estuary with a rippling current leading to a private ocean of fun and romance.

Then she jumped on a plane.

He often got impatient with the woman not being able to keep up with their own feelings, especially when their connection was so obvious. Nothing he could do about the timing in this case. He was determined not to smother her; just had to sit tight, let Sanaya lead with the level of communication she was comfortable with.

Maybe he had sent a few too many private messages via Facebook. He was a little nervous that her heading away so soon might cool off the sparks between them. She might even get homesick and decide to move back. On the positive, she was at a wedding, the most romantic event she could be at. Her cousin's joy might help breakdown that romance flippancy she so proudly threw at him; a shield she used to protect her heart.

She can't catch the wedding bouquet while holding a shield. Do they have bouquets in Hindu weddings? I'll ask her. If she ever responds to my messages!

A whole week after she had returned, there was still no response. Seven days. Three thick profile blue pens had doodled all their ink across half his large notebook. Ten days with sporadic mini communications, seven with none and no excuse. So he fired off another email:

*On the screen we watched our spiritual home… together in
our physical world… I saw the new moon last night and
it seemed to be winking… left me wondering what you
could see…*

It was exactly twenty-seven hours, thirty-three minutes, one more pen and a dozen pages wasted before he got a reply.

*All these messages that you send
When you have the option to phone a friend
I'm not here to play any game
But your phone technique is kinda lame.*

Leo laughed loud.

Sanaya wasn't just back, she was back on the ball. Her humor a good sign. She had even woven in another link to Slumdog with the 'phone a friend' bit. He pulled across the notebook and one of his favorite pens. Always blue. As a compulsive doodler he liked this pen because of the larger 1.4 sized ballpoint and the way the ink flowed on paper. He almost always started his creative ideas on a pad before typing them up. He needn't have bothered. This little verse poured out through the thick ink.

I don't play games when it comes to romance
There are enough challenges in this natural dance
That's not what I meant to imply
If you saw my phone bill you would die…

He typed up the poem in a text then hit send.

Sanaya laughed.

Why had she been procrastinating? In Mumbai, Leo musings danced around her everywhere. She cut her trip short to see him. Disappointed, no *devastated,* her mom. Arrived in Melbourne with no jetlag, full of energy and anticipation then hesitation.

Why?

Fear?

Was she afraid of diving deeper with Leo? *The dude's too consistently corny, too romantic to be a fake. I've never met a guy this comfortable talking about feelings... talking about everything and not always about him or sport.* Simply afraid of diving deeper? One of the advantages of boring guys was the dump-this-dude decision didn't take much effort, they clearly didn't deserve to soak up her precious time on this planet.

But Leo's different. Good different.

She picked up her phone and called him, sharing the stories of her trip, being careful not to fluff up the wedding stuff too much. By the end of the call, they had agreed on a dinner date and she'd hung up buzzing from the laughter and ease at which they had slipped back into their fun verbal sparring. But soon after, a heavy weight settled between her tummy and heart.

Sanaya slumped back, sitting cross-legged on her couch, an old pillow on her lap, picking at the embroidery. Embroidery stitched by her mom. In this almost meditative state, the reason for her procrastination floated into her mind like a neon sign. She released a sigh as long as a Melbourne winter. She couldn't avoid it any longer. This date she had to tell Leo the one bit of news she was sure he wouldn't want to hear. The age difference didn't bother her. His kids didn't bother her. But this might freak him out. Out of the restaurant, out of the relationship, out of her life.

9

SPOONING DESSERTS

Leo loved the intimacy of sharing dessert. Spooning the same cake had to be one of the most underrated sensual connections. The sweet and fruity Romate Muscatel had no chance of matching the triple chocolate concoction with vanilla ice-cream on the side that should have come with a card: *'do-not-pass-go, plunge directly into diabetes'*. His pancreas fought that battle while his heart soaked in the spirit of Sanaya. She'd removed her black leather jacket, revealing a spellbinding sleeveless blue dress with bright flowers creating an image of a secret tropical lagoon.

The iconic Spanish bar and restaurant, Movida, splashed with bricks and timber beams and modern artwork. Customers in the crowded booths and bustling bar created a noisy vibe, yet their small table in the lower section nestled into a cozy corner.

The mutual sensual ending to their meal simultaneously confirmed he and Sanaya had reached a level of comfort while also suggesting a step up in physical intimacy was close. *Maybe even tonight. Probably why she'd avoided my eyes a few times that evening. She's nervous.*

"I'm going to stay a virgin until I'm married," said Sanaya casually, like *'I'm going shopping tomorrow'*. But she studied his reaction with laser eyes.

He felt the words hanging in the air between them, in capitals and bold and underlined, threatening to collapse onto their wineglasses and half-finished cake.

I'M GOING TO STAY A VIRGIN UNTIL I'M MARRIED.

He put down his spoon and leaned back into the chair as he finished chewing the last chunk he'd shoveled into his mouth. A dietician would have been proud of his mastication as he slowed down to digest the ramification of Sanaya's statement. The longer he chewed, the more flavors and texture he uncovered.

"Wow, you must really like me. A lot." he said.

Sanaya's wide eyes and furrowed brow suggested that of all the potential responses she had rumbling around her brain, that wasn't one of them.

"Huh? What makes you say that?"

"Well, if you didn't like me. If you didn't maybe enjoy our kiss a few weeks ago... and maybe thinking about more than the kiss-"

"Enough with the ego." Sanaya rested her spoon on the plate and sat back. She'd aimed for her usual flippancy but couldn't hide the tenseness in her movements, her posture.

"This is a decision I made a few years ago and I will be sticking to it. It's not about you or any other specific man. It's something that I believe in and it is important to me."

Across the small table he felt her vulnerability and defiance. It wouldn't have been easy to share this honor driven mantra.

"I respect your decision and I wouldn't dare fight you on it or try to change your mind. It's just a surprise considering you said you were an atheist."

"It's not about religion. It's about my body and heart."

If he wasn't already falling in love with Sanaya before dessert, he was inexplicably free-falling now. The diverse layers made her a special soul. This only added to her uniqueness. And courage. He respected her strength to follow this path in a world that was swamped in media sexuality; dripping with artificial desire and mythical sexual utopia. Plus, she was following that path without the support of a church group. Not even family close by. It was her own thing.

But he did have a high sex drive.

It was one of the reasons he was so disciplined about keeping fit. The thousands of miles on bike tracks and the weekly tennis. More importantly, making love with someone he cared about was one of the most special things about a relationship. He often found it spiritual.

Sanaya moved the large empty dessert plate to the side and leaned forward over the table. He, took her outstretched hands; soft and warm. He wondered if sharing dessert was going to be the most intimate part of their relationship. The extreme boundary until... *Stop projecting Leo. She wants to say something else. Focus.* He leaned in towards Sanaya.

"I guess you don't feel like the rest of this," said Sanaya looking at the cake.

He smiled and pointed his spoon at the cake.

"If you think your virgin vows are going to stop me from eating more of this filthylicious cake, you don't know me well."

Sanaya smiled. "Filthylicious. I like that."

"Well, make up your mind."

She scrunched up her white cloth napkin and threw it at him.

He caught the napkin, folded it and returned it to her.

"I'm sorry. I'm not making fun of you. I respect your values and appreciate you bringing it up now."

Sanaya nodded, fiddled with the napkin then put it on the table.

"You don't need to answer this tonight. Actually, I don't want you to answer this tonight. But I need to know, eventually... based on what I've told you... do you still want to... to share another dessert?"

❧

"That's got to be a deal breaker, yeah?" said Paul.

The sunlight streaked through the mix of gum and pine trees on the east side of the aqueduct track above Eltham. It created a gentle strobe effect as Paul and Leo cycled along at a steady fifteen miles per hour. They were riding side by side now after conquering the long hill to get to this relatively flat section. Somehow, Paul was always on Leo's right hand side. It was heading to a warm, autumn day, the kind Melbourne often teases with leading up to Easter before winter unleashes.

"There are so many layers in this, Paul," he said as he leaned down to put his drink bottle back in its holder. "You know me, I've always been open to marrying again, so Sanaya bringing up the idea of marriage so early isn't a deal breaker."

They closed in on a jogger. He rang his bell to not startle her and Paul let him push forward as they passed her single file. Paul then cruised up on his right again.

"Sexual compatibility is such a critical thing for me. But how do you know you are sexually compatible if you don't have sex until after you marry?"

"I remember that singer you went out with. She really got into your heart but it wasn't happening in bed, yeah."

"Yes, JJ had an amazing voice but we couldn't do harmonies."

"Yeah, singing has never really been your thing, yeah." Said Paul.

"Ha ha. But I would never have picked it, see. That's the scary thing. She was sexy, creative, fun… when it came to sex, we were all over the place, but never in the same zone."

They rode in silence for a hundred yards.

"What about that Muslim woman? You handled her well."

"That's because I didn't handle her."

They both laughed then passed an elderly couple

walking their poodle. But Paul had raised someone relevant. Rukia was an intelligent Iraqi refugee who dressed like a modern westerner and embraced her new country while clinging to some of her Islamic beliefs. The key one being they could date but there would be no touching. For tactile Leo, this was a massive challenge. However, it quickly became liberating. Because physical contact wasn't even on the menu, they never had to navigate the right time to progress the relationship through the sometimes messy map of physical intimacy.

After a couple of months of dating and not crossing the line, Rukia dumped him. It wasn't ugly, just unexpected as everything between them was flowing well. Six months later she called him again. At the first new date, she told him he was the only one that had abided by her rule.

"What about Muslim men?" he'd asked.

"They were the worst." She almost spat the words out.

At the end of that date, *she* broke the no-touching rule. Over the next few weeks their intimacy crossed many borders but not the big check-point. One night, when it seemed inevitable their passion had to crash through the final barrier, she dropped another bombshell.

"Leo, we can't do this unless you become a Muslim."

That didn't just pour cold water on the steamy moment, it dumped a glacier on the whole relationship. As an atheist, this was too much; he was willing to accept Rukia's beliefs. Hell, he was even happy to give up bacon and alcohol. To suddenly convert to Islam was one relationship bridge too far for him. It didn't matter what religion she was. Plus, he wasn't impressed with the timing.

At least Sanaya raised her situation early. There wasn't any hint of manipulation.

Leo swerved to avoid a tiny dog and gave the dog's owner a glare as they zoomed past because too many people didn't take care of their pets on shared tracks.

"You're right, Paul. My relationship with Rukia proved I am able to adapt if I really care about the woman. Plus, Sanaya isn't asking me to join a religion or cult."

They neared the part of the track where they detoured for a steep downhill road section. Last time down he set a new speed record of forty-eight miles an hour. The ever-competitive Paul had edged him, hitting fifty miles. It was a risky sprint and they had to feel right about going flat-out. Sometimes they just cruised down.

"Going for it?" asked Paul.

Leo nodded, turned his bike onto the steep road then plunged downhill. He had some control over a potential new speed record, but absolutely no idea about the uncharted romantic track Sanaya had flung them on.

10

THE MOVIDA VIRGIN VOWS

Dinner at my place Saturday?

Sanaya stared at Leo's text message as her dancing buddies bundled out of the dance studio. She looked up at the mirrored wall; pulled up her favorite loose purple linen pants and pulled down the red t-shirt with Indian-like patterns in white and orange. Her breathing still heavy from the ninety-minute Bollywood class, forehead shiny with perspiration

Dinner at my place Saturday?

Five words, five days after her virgin statement. Was this Leo accepting her situation or wanting to lure her into an environment that would test her resolve? Should she call him to be absolutely clear, or just assume the best? After all, he had taken time to consider it as she asked, and there he was inviting her to dinner at his place. That had to be his way of saying he's okay with it. She sent him a text to test the simmering waters.

What's for dessert?

Leo must have been waiting for her response because her phone pinged with a message alert by the time she'd picked up her bag and taken a couple of steps towards the door. She scrambled to find her phone from the bottom of her messy backpack.

Something filthylicious.

And a smiley face emoji.

Her laughter bounced around the empty gym.

Thank the spirits for his sense of humor. Even if it's a bit lame sometimes. This moment could have been much worse with the wrong guy. Then again, with the wrong guy, she wouldn't have had to share her commitment to virginity.

At least he'd picked a nice restaurant for her bombshell. Movida wasn't cheap and you had to book weeks in advance. None of her other dates had lasted long enough to make the booking. The closeness of tables and boisterous energy had reminded her a little of Mumbai.

She'd never forget Leo's face when she'd dumped her virgin vow on him. He couldn't hide his initial shock, but the dude kept chewing that cake, then his eyes sparkled again, then he smiled. Chewing and smiling turned him into a scary clown.

She laughed.

Sanaya's laughter competed with the Gypsy Kings on Leo's CD player, the squeals of next door's two young boys and the cockatoos squeaking through the sliding screen door.

Leo had just shown her a picture from his 21st birthday party; an old fashioned printed photo. She found it hilarious on two levels. Firstly, the sight of Leo with his hair permed in tight curls, rather than his flowing wavy locks.

The second juicy piece of magic captured in this colored bit of history, was the naked blow-up doll he had his arm around. With his tight light-brown shirt undone almost to his belly button and classic silver mug in his left hand, he was obviously mid-speech. His dad was laughing on one side while his mom was in shock on the other, like she was trying to push the doll under the table.

"It's true. My close friends gave me a nice watch and the doll. They christened the doll Wendy. Next Wendy I met, I married."

"Familiarity," she said.

They both laughed.

"But your hair! You look like a seventies playboy."

"Eighties Casanova. Perming my hair was one of the three big times I let down my ultra-conservative Italian parents."

"Did they ask you to straighten it?"

"Mom pleaded with me, but dad was... let's say he was more creative."

"How?" said Sanaya.

"He was out when I first came home with the perm. I was in the lounge room watching TV with everyone, my mom almost in tears with sadness. My baby sister worried about what dad would do to me. My younger brother looking forward to what dad would do to me. Then we heard dad arrive downstairs. Everyone tensed up. They all knew he was going to lose it. He didn't have a regular temper, but when he lost it, he really lost it."

"So what did he do?" said Sanaya concerned.

"He walked to the door, saw me, stared at my hair for a few seconds... said nothing and turned back out."

"Well, that's okay."

"That's what I thought. Before I tell you the rest, I have to point out that before you came to Australia, Fitzroy Street in St Kilda wasn't all trendy cafes, restaurants and bars like today. It used to be the center for junkies and hookers – male and female. Quite seedy."

"Right," said Sanaya.

"So dad comes back thirty seconds later with one of mom's biggest hand bags. He threw it at me then yelled; *'Now you can go to Fitzroy Street with all the other poofters'*."

They both laughed so loud, the cockatoos outside were spooked and flew off in a flutter.

Sanaya isn't sure exactly when it happened, but sometime during that night there was a seismic shift which let Leo walk right up to the front door of her heart. She could hear him knocking with a deep double-tap like a fast Bollywood beat; actually that *was* her heart pumping.

Maybe it was how easily he had accepted her virginity vow. When she'd arrived he made her sit at his dining table. He placed an unopened bar of Haigh's dark mint chocolate on the table, got down on one knee and placed his right hand on the chocolate, his left on top of her hands on her lap. "I hereby swear, on my favorite chocolate, that I fully understand and accept the Movida Virgin Vows."

She didn't know whether to laugh or cry. The tears didn't wait for permission.

"I respect your beliefs fully and will not, under any circumstances, attempt to break the Movida Virgin Vows". He kissed her hands. "Are you okay?"

The silly and beautiful little ceremony gave her a jalebi heart, sweet and syrupy and curled around her soul. She smiled through her tears and nodded.

"Good, I've got stuff to do in the kitchen." Leo spun away. Then spun back again. She wiped the tears rolling down her cheeks.

"You're so beautiful. Like a stunning sun shower." He bent down and kissed her gently on the cheek. He licked her tears. Slowly at first, then more exaggerated, like an excited puppy. Sanaya laughed and pushed him away.

"Go cook. You're obviously hungry."

Maybe it was just having a man cook for her; there was something sexy about a man getting busy in the kitchen just for her. He kept emphasizing he was no gourmet chef, that he just cooked basic food. But he *was cooking for her,* and no man had done that before. Apart from her dad, which didn't count.

Leo prepared a prawn salad the way his dad had taught him. With a little olive oil, a touch of garlic, parsley from his garden, sprinkled with finely chopped chilies, and a dash of lemon. It was delicious. Together with the balsamic vinegar based dressing for the accompanying garden salad, it was healthy too. The dessert was borderline healthy. Sliced strawberries and mango mixed in maple syrup and fresh lime juice, topped with a scattering of small broken pieces of mint dark chocolate. Just as Leo promised, *filthylicious.*

Her seismic shift could have happened through any of their crazy laughter, her resistance to love and romance bumped away, buried in the rubble of skepticism.

Or it might have snuck in while they were slow dancing in Leo's lounge room. He'd changed the mood to Patricia Kaas, a French pop-jazz singer. They didn't understand the French lyrics, but they didn't need to; her husky voice and slinky melodies transcended language. The flat screen TV and sound system guarded one corner, two couches at a right angle protected the opposite corner; creating a natural dance floor on the polished timber boards. Next to the couch and small wooden coffee table, a high artificial tree had its leaves covered with tiny colored lights, adding to the atmosphere with the red lamp on the table.

Somehow the mixture of furniture and lighting worked. He hadn't put a stray hand where it didn't belong for over thirty minutes of fun slow-dancing;

sensual and romantic, safe and exhilarating all at the same time.

❧

It had taken all of Leo's will power to keep his hands honest and his lips on a self-imposed temporary intervention order. He was determined to show Sanaya he meant what he said with her Movida Virgin Vows. It wasn't just a silly ceremony he'd thought up for fun or diversion. He even told a white lie for the cause when she asked him what the title of the Patricia Kaas CD meant, 'Dans ma Chair'. There was no way that he was going to tell her it meant 'In my Flesh'; safer to say he didn't know.

Then she kissed him.

A slow passionate kiss that outlasted the length of the final song. They kept dancing through the kiss. Burning through the kiss. Melting through the kiss. When the CD ended, she didn't pull away, her lips and tongue wild; like it was the first time she'd ever kissed a man and was going to swallow him whole. Thousands of years of biology, all his forty-eight years of instincts, every fiber and muscle in his body screamed to spin Sanaya around, nibble on the back of her neck, let his hands explore her flesh under her silky blouse.

Sanaya pulled her head back, black eyes a misty galaxy, breathing heavy, warm. He took her hand and led her to his bedroom.

She hesitated at the doorway.

"Trust me," said Leo.

◈

Trust me...

Back home, Sanaya lay on her bed, clothes and shoes still on, bag flopped on the floor, wide eyes and New-York-never-going-to-sleep-body. Her permanent grin projected the images of every single micro-moment onto the ceiling.

Trust me...

She trusted Leo's eyes more than she trusted herself. She'd entered a man's bedroom for the first time in the safety of a feeling she couldn't define or understand. Leo sat her down on the edge of the bed. Then he stood in front of her, framed in tight blue chinos and a blue-burgundy Ben Sherman shirt with the long sleeves folded a couple of times. He turned around and lit half a dozen candles on the dressing table which flickered like dozens against the large mirror. His chinos outlining perfection as he bent over to light the final candle. She floated on flames.

Leo joined her on the bed. Part of her was more alive and in the moment than she'd ever been, part of her spirit observed like a guardian angel. His slow, heavy breaths were in rhythm with hers. Even under the low lighting, she could see the passion and care in his eyes. He gently ran the back of his right fingers down her right cheek, slowly under her lip then opened his hand over her left cheek, flowing his fingers over her ear, through her hair. Leo gently encouraged her to lay back.

Skin and nerves competed for attention all over her pulsating body. She let him guide her down. She stopped breathing for a moment as Leo delicately moved some hair that had fallen across her face. Her lips just wanted more of his. He must've read her mind and kissed her.

Over the next couple of hours they kissed passionately, hugged, rolled, giggled and talked about their dreams, often curled up in Leo's arms. All clothes stayed where they started. All hands behaved. Just. But inside both of their bodies there were riots and carnivals; it was impossible to miss Leo's outward excitement but he honored her vow and didn't put a finger wrong. Yet, it was still the sexiest moment of her life. The most in-the-moment moment of her life.

I want to learn everything about you, one dream at a time.

Leo smiled at Sanaya's text. It was half time at his son's soccer match the day after the amazing night before. Even though it was his 'free' weekend, he usually took Thomas to his games. It wasn't much of a performance so far. He hadn't expected much from the first practice match of the season. Plus, Thomas was a special talent and you could see he was bored out there. He'd previously coached 16-year-old Thomas and his eldest son, James, for four years each. But now he was enjoying just being a soccer-dad. Joey was satisfying his 12-year-old taste buds at the canteen—probably with his usual coke and dim-sims, despite the warm, late March day.

He typed a response to Sanaya on his iPhone.

I want to walk around the world with you, one beach at a time.

He turned on the volume to make sure he caught her reply as soon as it came through, at least till the game re-started. He always had his phone on silent while Thomas or any of his boys were playing. When he was watching them, he was watching them. He didn't have to wait long. As he stood up to stretch his legs and relieve his numbing backside from the steel backless bench seat his phone chirped.

We can always meet in our memories, one night at a time.

Her words entered through his eyes, flooded the right side of his brain, zinged through his heart and veins, then tumbled out of his fingers with an instant reply.

I wait to see your smile again, one breath at a time.

He loved this mutual-muse aspect of their relationship. They had launched their romantic rocket with poetry and continued orbiting in their own Milky Way, fueled by each other's creative juices. He put his phone back on silent as the players came out and Joey returned with his junk food. Leo was glad that none of his boys had a metabolism that was ever going to take them near the 'obese' league. They were lucky. He watched Thomas closely as he came out of the dressing rooms. A few other parents yelled encouragement to their sons. Leo was relaxed. Thomas finally had his game face on; his coach had pushed the right buttons. Twenty minutes later Rovers were 3-nil up. Thomas had scored two and set up one; after that he just drifted around the pitch again, game face packed away.

. . .

Leo turned off his bedside lamp but couldn't resist picking up his mobile to read their poetic text trail again.

I want to learn everything about you, one dream at a time.
I want to walk around the world with you, one beach at a time.
We can always meet in our memories, one night at a time.
I wait to see your smile again, one breath at a time.

Maybe they weren't art, but they were original and organic. Their words. Inspired by each other, written to each other. He'd never been with a woman like Sanaya, one who was equally poetic and romantic. So many women pine about sailing on a sea of romance with a guy, but they always have some baggage dangling in the water like an anchor.

Once he'd guided Sanaya out of her safe harbor, she sailed her mainsail fully set on a mast of fun.

11

PICNIC SURPRISE

The following Friday night Sanaya torpedoed new words into their romantic yacht, blasting their relationship out of the cruisy sea of fun.

"What do you care about my mom? You're only with me till a woman comes along who will open her legs."

The words cannoned around Leo's head like a bunch of marbles dropped in a steel bucket, jarring on so many levels. The shock of hearing them from Sanaya. The fiery tone. Plus, hearing 'my mom in the same sentence.

Interesting conversation for a romantic evening picnic. A couple of years ago he would've instantly slipped into defensive mode. Maybe even resorted back to passive aggressive. An unfortunate phase he slumped into when he let his ex-wife trip him into a downward spiral because of how she used their children as weapons. At the time, he projected his frustration at his romantic partner, Kali. She was wise enough to sense the anger wasn't his natural state and recommended he do some therapy.

After initially being defensive about the suggestion, he became grateful for her courage in seeing and calling his anger. He found a terrific therapist and three months later had gained more mindfulness than he had ever expected going in. The therapy also finally inspired him to begin meditation and study Buddhism, two things he had been interested in exploring for a long time. Unfortunately, Kali wanted a baby and their relationship ended just before Leo's first therapy session.

With heavy relationship experience under his belt, and invaluable therapy, Leo found himself in a zen-like moment, studying Sanaya's barely recognizable pained face with her normally full red lips rolled into each other, like she was trying to stop anymore venom seeping out, furrowed brow an extension of the lips.

"I care about you, therefore, I care about your mom." His soft even tone was a relief. Her mom had just lost her art teaching job. At her age, and the rare budgets for art at schools in Mumbai, the odds for replacing it were low.

"You care about me now." A defiance in her voice as she picked at the band aid on the tip of her left pointing finger.

"Now is all we know," said Leo.

"I should have thought things through before starting this silly game. Before we kissed. You've been with so many women, I'm just another one on your conveyor belt."

He didn't think they'd get to the chocolate that was

staying cool in the Esky. He'd gone into the city earlier that day to get some of his favorites from Haigh's. The distraction of the chocolate inspired another distraction, and any distraction had to be sweeter than where Sanaya had steered the conversation.

"Anyway, your mom and I have a special bond."

Sanaya's lips uncurled. There was no smile or grin, but she was blessed with a disposition that oozed joy, so this was a big step forward.

"I should never have told you about that," she said.

Leo and Sanaya's mom shared the same birthday; ten years older but still, that's special. He'd only met two other people who shared that milestone. An avocado dip that he'd made lay next to the plate of Sanaya's roti, and a plastic container with sliced carrot, capsicum and celery. Their wine glasses balanced on the Esky lid, provided prisms for the city lights. He'd chosen this secluded hill on Yarra Boulevard because it gave a stunning view of the city skyline. A cool night but no breeze.

Was Sanaya struggling with inner turmoil around her Movida Virgin Vows? Was the vow a promise to her mom? Why else drag her mom into the conversation that way? He'd met too many women who had major issues with their mother. He wasn't wise enough to know what triggered Sanaya's outburst. She had maneuvered herself to a corner of the blanket on the high side. Her knees scrunched up to her chest, arms wrapped tight around her black jeans. If she flipped the brown hood of her sweater onto her head, you might think she was a defensive street-kid.

"Shall we pack up?" he said.

Sanaya nodded.

⁂

No matter how far Leo's car might've been moving away from the scene of her crime, Sanaya's mood stuck like the wine stain on the picnic blanket. No idea what had stirred up her verbal-vomit. Deflated. Disappointed she spoiled the date. She'd challenged Leo to come up with something simple but different because she was determined not to fall into the habit of always ending up at his place, and she wasn't ready to bring him to her apartment. He brought them to the hill on the side of Yarra Boulevard in Kew. It wasn't even an official park but surprised her with the spectacular view of the city. Her internal view was the opposite; a dark painful catastrophe. She understood the feelings jabbing at her.

But why did I say those horrible, ugly words.

They'd packed in silence, avoiding eye contact and any touching. Wished she could curl up and hide in the cold Esky.

When Leo dropped her off, Sanaya opened her door almost before the car stopped. He opened his door as well.

"Please don't," she said, needing the night to end. She couldn't swing from the pit of embarrassment and confusion to affection.

Leo reluctantly closed his door.

"You can have the roti," she said, pointing at the

Esky on the back seat, before she swiveled out of her seat.

"Goodnight, Sanaya."

She swung the door shut and scurried into her building.

After she had scrambled into her apartment, Sanaya plonked herself at the table and tried to sort out what was going on in her stupid head.

Ajala.

Her cousin had called the night before and dropped a meteor onto her world, knocking everything into a shaky spin.

"So, have you let your sexy Leo discover your inner lioness?" said Ajala.

"Ajuuuu!" Sanaya laughed loud. Aju always made her laugh. "I'm sticking to our gupt sandhi."

"Oh Sany, we were just sixteen. Please do not tell me you are stuck on that silly promise we made."

She'd been lying down on the couch but sprang into a sitting position. Feel-good humor ran off with her physical comfort.

"But we swore to Shakti," she said.

Silence. She checked her phone screen and the call was still live.

"Aju?"

"And we swore we'd travel the world together," said Ajala.

True, born just a few months apart, her bond with Ajala

had been unbreakable. Ajala had been the sister she never had, her closest friend. But Sanaya had announced she was going to study in Australia. Then she decided Melbourne would be her home. She was the one who'd abandoned Ajala. A swallow landed on her lounge room window sill, a naturally communal bird perched comfortably on its own.

"I'm sorry Aju, I…"

"Forget it, Sany. We are both solo spirits. That's why we connected, to help us survive the crowd. I love my life here and you're being brave down there."

"I don't feel brave, and for the first time I feel…confused."

"Listen, Sany, you're amazing. If you want to stay a virgin till marriage, I support you one hundred percent. Just don't do it because you feel you owe me for that promise. Do it because that's what you believe is right for you."

Sanaya slumped into the couch, didn't know what to believe anymore. When Leo innocently tested her commitment to her virgin vows, it was her pact with Ajala that had kept her strong.

"Sany, are you okay?"

"Yes, yes." She sat on the edge of the couch, a surge of curiosity returned strength to her body. "Aju, you didn't wait until your wedding night?"

Silence.

"After you were engaged?"

Silence.

"Aju, we never have to speak about this again, but we made that vow together, I deserve to know."

"Before we were engaged, but after I knew he loved me."

"Okay, thank you," said Sanaya. *After I knew he loved me.* That was something.

"He wasn't the first," whispered Ajala.

"What! Aju, you have more surprises than the Hindi have festivals."

"I am the Festival of Ajala."

Sanaya exploded with laughter.

Post Leo date, Sanaya sat at the dining table, emotions clunking and spinning inside her like forgotten coins in a clothes dryer.

I should've cancelled the date.

That's what her intuition had whispered all day. She'd actually typed and deleted the text twice. *Let's give tonight a miss. I'll call you soon.* Delete. She'd turn back to reading "The Hunger Games" but her mind kept drifting, morphing the characters with reality. She had closed the book and imagined being Katniss. Was Leo her Gale, a man who would never return her simmering love? Or is Leo a Peeta, someone that helps her survive for a while and maybe helps her learn some new skills along the way? *If I'm confused about this…I shouldn't be with him.* She threw the book on the couch next to her, snatched her phone and typed.

This isn't going to work. Can't come tonight. I'll call you. She had stared at the words for ages. Ages. He's forty-eight, I'm twenty-eight. He's got three kids. Three. I could date his oldest son and not be tagged a cougar.

The screen on her iPhone was small, the letters tiny, the message huge.

This isn't going to work. Can't come tonight. I'll call you.

Sanaya read it three times, maybe four.

Deleted it.

There was no way she could focus on any book. Her brain couldn't harness the conflict in her head or release the tightness in her body. She was drawn to the one thing that always helped her escape, emptied her mind and freed her muscles. She turned the Bollywood cd on high volume and practiced her upcoming performance routine. The limited space between the couch and kitchen table wasn't ideal but she had thrown herself into every inch with an intensity that made ninety-minutes feel like nine.

In her post-dance spiritual high, fueled by large doses of endorphins, she realized there was less than an hour until Leo's pick up time. Not much time to shower, make-up and choose clothes. Plus, she had to slice the vegetables too.

That brought Sanaya back to the mess on the kitchen bench. And the bloodied tissues from cutting her finger earlier when a stubborn carrot rolled. Another bad sign. She stared at the band-aid on her left finger, fraying at the edges after all her subconscious fiddling.

I should have cancelled. Spent some time with Lakshmi.

She stared at the little table by the door dedicated to small statute of Lakshmi. Lakshmi with four hands.

I need four brains to work out my stupid, stupid, stupidity. Or four hearts... so I don't hurt Leo again. Again? Why would the dude want to be anywhere near me again? I don't want to be near me.

She straightened in the chair, eyes glued on Lakshmi. This wasn't just about her. She'd lashed out at Leo. Hurt him. She didn't recognize his eyes; not just the sudden dullness, something else. On a different scale from when she'd dumped the Movida Virgin Vows on him. Was it fear? Disappointment? Heartbreak? She trundled to the couch, picked up her favorite big cushion, plonked it on the floor in front of Lakshmi and sat on it cross legged.

'*Self-pity serves no soul*'. One of her dad's mantras.

She would sit with Lakshmi, meditate and ruminate until she understood her actions without judgment and worked out the kindest way forward for her and Leo. Even if that meant ending the relationship. If it wasn't already too late. She closed her eyes. "*In with the good*" she said internally as she inhaled deep into her belly. "*Out with the bad.*" As she exhaled. Then breathed in deep again, "*In with acceptance…Out with anger…In with my love…Out with fear…*" She repeated her mantra until the words floated quietly in the back of her mind and she centered with her breath.

12

PRINCESS TOWER

Leo untied the hood on his Adidas spray jacket and flipped it back without slowing his stride up the Westerfolds Park hill. Cool morning air hit his neck and ears below the Arsenal cap, but the showers had finally stopped. Light rain had ruled out a bike ride and he needed to release energy, plus he enjoyed walking in the rain. Especially when he wasn't enjoying the factious storylines filling his head.

A heart pumping from exercise is healthier than a heart racing in anxiety or drowning in sorrow.

Sanaya's anxiety the previous night wasn't a shock, the language and finality was. He'd come across the same anxiety before in some of his relationships and his friends' sad stories. Sometimes it was driven by women who had lingering abandonment issues. Other times they were irrational moments of insecurity as they projected forward. Occasionally the lashing out was conscious and calculated, but usually impulsive. Whatever the reasons, Sanaya feared being dumped, so she pushed him away first. The key question haunted him: was it a preliminary booking for her fight-or-flight departure or was she already flying.

At the top of the hill, he pulled his phone out to check the timing, the walk from his place usually took twenty-five minutes to reach the summit. He didn't even register the clock, the SMS alert from Sanaya took all his focus.

Can you meet today at Albert Park Lake, 3pm?

No explanation, no apology, no emotion.

But three good omens; any communication is better than none, in person is a million times more effective and compassionate than any other modern tech-messy option, and she'd chosen Albert Park Lake, one of his favorite spots in the world – from his dad driving them there every Sunday morning for six months when he'd started playing soccer as a ten-year-old, to hundreds of runs and walks as an adult, the lake had become a spiritual zone - although he'd never told Sanaya.

He replied '*Yes*', turned the ring volume on and squeezed the phone back into his jeans pocket, then admired the view to the west, including the peaks of the highest down-town buildings. Trees glistened in the foreground; no sun yet, but the clouds had shifted higher, lighter. He did his three basic stretches, hamstrings, quads and calves which at his age also stretched the hips. Raised his arms in a slow circle as he breathed in and out; halfway through the second circle his phone pinged. He breathed out and checked the text.

Sanaya, confirmed the exact location.

Another good omen. He shoved the phone back and headed down the hill.

Leo parked further away than he needed to and soaked in the palm trees and tranquility. The man-made Albert Park Lake was surrounded by a four mile walking and running track, parkland, playgrounds and sports grounds. For ten months of the year a beautiful oasis on the edge of the CBD; the other two, a chaotic noisy epicenter for the Melbourne F1 Grand Prix, from the construction of grandstands and sponsor marquis and the four-day event, to dismantling everything back to the peaceful normality.

He ambled along the lake path past the boatsheds, past the parents worshipping coffee cups at the kiosk, and beelined around the children preparing for sailing lessons on the little dinghies. The feel good atmosphere of this section jostled in his gut with the tension of the purpose. Meeting Sanaya. What was his purpose within that purpose? His inner reaction to Sanaya's Movida Virgin Vows turned out okay, that potential obstacle helped build their romantic bond. Her attack last night had an edge so sharp it hacked through the bond. Questions swirled in his head: was it a rare outburst or is this her pattern? Sweet and romantic one minute, insecure and aggressive the next. Did he want to end the short romance today on good terms or risk being battered by her pattern? Was this ever going to be more than a fling? Well, it's never been a *fling* because it wasn't sexual.

He spotted Sanaya at the top of the steel viewing tower, twenty yards high on the northwest edge of the lake. He almost tripped, stopped, took in a long breath which came out as an even longer sigh. She was facing the opposite direction, but there was no mistaking her black hair and almost childish hunching on the railing. It was always breezy here, close to the bay, but the autumn sun was kindly throwing a supportive shine during its usual Melbourne window of warmth between two and four in the afternoon. After that, it would get cool fast.

It took a little time to catch his breath after climbing the spiral stairs. Her radiant smile was back and that had to be a good sign. Sanaya was wearing a red cardigan over a black t-shirt, black jeans and red sneakers.

"You chose this spot so you can push me over?" said Leo.

Sanaya laughed, didn't sound forced. She peered over the edge. A couple in their twenties ran underneath heading counterclockwise with all their branded gear, swans on the lake looked small, the ducks tiny.

"It's one of my favorite places," said Sanaya.

"Mine, too." He relaxed a little. He thought it was a good omen when she suggested this location but tried not to project too fast – his usual relationship mistake – because the previous night had spooked him. Maybe her age finally showed an immaturity he didn't want to see. Walking towards the tower, he couldn't help his brain tossing around potential scenarios. He wasn't sure what to expect.

"Last night you were amazing," said Sanaya.

He hadn't expected that.

"I said some stupid things. Awful things. Yet you didn't flinch. You never got angry. You were gentle with me." There was a warm kindness in her voice; his soul welcomed it with an invisible hug.

"I'm sorry, Leo. I hope you can forgive me."

"Wow," said Leo, "that was such a beautiful thing for you to say." And extremely mature. So much for his temporary heightened concern about her age.

"Of course I forgive you."

Two swans glided by below them, his heart christened by the lake and Sanaya's words. No going back now. If they could get through such an ugly hiccup so quickly and gently, he was convinced they could get through anything. He was a born-again-romantic, in love with Sanaya.

❧

Leo's open happy face unwound Sanaya's tummy and her hands relaxed their grip on the railing. No questions, no hesitation. Instant forgiveness. How could she not fall in love with this guy?

He opened his arms and she stepped inside. She hugged him tight, eyes closed. He hugged back, gently squeezing her mutual fear, molding it into relief and letting it drift away with long, deep sighs. She lifted her head from his chest and floated in his eyes. His lips parted and that opened up a valve in her. She leaned up and kissed him. When they pulled their heads back they both smiled. It felt like a new first kiss. Maybe because they both thought their short romance was over just eighteen hours ago. Or maybe the height added some vertigo. Whatever it was, Sanaya didn't want to risk missing those lips, or the way he wrapped her up in his arms.

"You are like a princess in this tower."

"So, you are my shining knight? Ready to slay the dragons?"

"I was ready to tickle a few swans, maybe shoo some ducks away. One sight of a dragon and you'd be on your own, babe."

"Ha. If you call me 'babe' again, you will be on your own."

She spun around and faced the lake, flung her hair over one shoulder and leant into the railing. Leo snuggled up behind her, sliding his hands around her waist. He kissed her neck slowly and then rested his cheek next to hers. Sanaya melted into every sensitive caress of his lips, every pore of his skin on hers. How silly she had been.

After her inexplicable, almost inexcusable lashing out at Leo last night she had had a horrible sleep. Her subconscious tortured with a mashing of Hunger Games; she fought battles with spears, arrows, and her messy clothes drawers. She fled from tributes and crushed heart-shaped rocks with her hands. Chaotic nightmares fueled by her fear of not knowing how to love someone, or more accurately, how to accept Leo's love.

A shaft of sunlight which had found a way through the gap in the old curtains and streamed across her bed shined some inner-clarity. It was like Leo had snuck into her room while she was sleeping and rummaged through her feelings. Instead of leaving a mess, all her things were neatly in their place. For the first time since she left Mumbai, maybe the first time in her life, she felt not just at home in her new town, she belonged. Her sailing soul had thrown down an anchor in safe waters, Lake Leo.

The next two weeks flew by with a number of dates that were fun and relaxed. Sanaya had let go of the romantic reins she was gripping and stopped rationing her time with Leo. Two moments in particular stood out for her.

The Saturday following her Princess Tower moment, Leo had driven them up to the Dandenongs, on the eastern edge of Melbourne. She had never been up there, even though it was only a forty-five minute drive from the CBD. The winding Mount Dandenong Tourist road revealed a visual feast around each bend. Picturesque forests of towering pine trees, gum trees, lush green ferns and glorious flowers.

Her favorite spot was Smits & Bits in Sassafras. Hidden off the main road, the short walk down the entrance laneway opened up into a fairy tale courtyard that could have been the center pages of a picture book.

Leo must have been expecting a reaction from her because he had his iPhone camera ready and captured her joyous smile.

A large maple tree provided a protective umbrella over most of the space. An L-shaped balcony full of cute trinkets separated the courtyard and the cottage store. There seemed to be a million unique gifts and plaques with beautiful or witty words. Sanaya and Leo enjoyed a moment on the bench swing, rocking gently and looking up through the maple branches and leaves as the sun playfully tried to shoo away the clouds.

Later, as they had enjoyed the traditional tea and fresh scones in the cafe next door, she realized Leo and her mom were indeed kindred spirits. It wasn't just a birthday they shared. Her mom would have loved the earthy space of Smits and Bits. It wasn't the kind of thing you'd expect a man to enjoy. They even shared a sugar habit as she watched Leo ignore the cream but swathe his scone with a thick layer of the yummy homemade strawberry jam. He looked ten years younger under the black pageboy cap which framed his eyes with the greenish-brown cotton scarf, beaming childlike joy as he gorged on the scone.

Leo saw her staring and he smiled while chewing, creating his scary clown look again. She laughed. That silly face always made her laugh. Through the large window with white timber crisscrossing, the sun lit up his left side.

"Hey, Moonface," she said as she wiped a bit of jam on his chin.

"Hey, Sunface."

He stopped eating, sat back. "No woman's ever christened me with a nickname."

Or vice-versa. Sanaya cherished this little 'first'. She also loved her nickname. It wasn't something she would have predicted two and half months ago. Nor this special day. *How many men would enjoy meandering around a shop like that?* A whole day of shops in fact. If she compared that date with food, she'd call it a slow cooked meal. No rush. A timeless sensation of being together in a beautiful part of the world. Comfort food for the soul.

෯

The day after the Sassafras trip, she went to Leo's for lunch. It was grey and pouring outside, but warm in his house. When they finished the simple but tasty chicken stir-fry, Leo stood behind her chair. He gently worked her head backwards with his hands then leaned down and kissed her. The super sensual Spider-man moment launched, a passionate afternoon that ended up on the plush red rug.

At no time was she ever going to weaken on her Movida Virgin Vows. But every second her body ached and pleaded internally for more. She knew she crossed the line a little by allowing Leo to caress her breast through her satin blouse. She also knew she couldn't entirely blame his persistent hands. Fiery hands.

While Leo's hands were doing the exploring, it was Sanaya who made the discoveries. Enjoying sensations from her anatomy in a way she never had before. Her inner nature permeated her sensual soul without any external penetration.

In the end, her only escape was literally a cold shower; she flung open the sliding door, ran into the backyard, and was drenched in the cool autumn rain within seconds. She spread her arms wide, arched her back, closed eyes facing the clouds, releasing an explosive laugh. Leo's laughter opened her eyes. Infectious, huskier than she'd ever heard him, they ended up on their knees on the wet grass, giggling uncontrollably. The rain couldn't wash away his cheeky eyes and smile. She adored him.

That night, lying in her bed alone, Sanaya kept her hands above the quilt. She had learned something about herself; there was a point of no return. A culmination of moments and touches that can lead you into a river of the sweetest, most intoxicating juices. You couldn't just dip your toe in this river, the raging currents beneath the surface wrap their power around all of you. Much more than her imagination or any book or movie was capable of simulating. It was like a drowning that created the opposite of death. Made her body more alive than ever. Her virginity had almost drowned in those juices that day. But she had survived and now she knew how far she could not go.

She was proud of herself, still grinning, while the currents from the afternoon continued flowing through her. She was, however, curious about Leo's heat-seeker hands, he seemed to have his own sustainable power source. Leo-thermal heat.

She laughed.

Maybe one day, she'd let him give her a massage, with her underwear on of course, and a big thick towel covering critical bits. That would be something. But not for a while. It didn't take much to encourage this guy! Besides she had a busy week.

❧

Driving home after dropping off Sanaya, Leo's body was buzzing. Rocket booster buzzing.

He'd been lucky to have experienced some amazing sexual moments, raw, erotic and spiritual, but that day with Sanaya spun sensuality into another galaxy; all without taking their clothes off. If they could harness the heat radiating from their bodies on his lounge room floor they'd become billionaires in supplying sustainable energy.

Then the crazy woman ran out into the cold rain.

Drenched on his back lawn the rain wasn't enough to drown the sexual energy roaring through their bodies and they exploded in an orgasm of laughter. Her deep guttural howls archived in his memory forever.

Back inside the house he'd given Sanaya a huge bath towel that completely covered her still clothed body. Sanaya looked sexier than ever with stringy wet hair stuck to her cheeks. He hoped the soaking might lead to a clichéd movie moment where she removed her clothes, or took a shower and deliberately left the bathroom door open.

Luckily for Sanaya, bad luck for him, she'd been shopping in the city before taking the bus to Leo's house and she had new jeans and a zip-up jacket to throw on. He lent her a t-shirt and respected her request for privacy as she changed in the bathroom.

While he drove her home through the pounding rain, they didn't say a word and often burst into giggles. He was proud of his discipline so far. His respect of Sanaya's wishes. But he was also sure that they would soon consummate their relationship. There was no doubt she enjoyed the day. Every kiss and caress. Every contortion their legs and craving bodies created. It was just a matter of time.

13

RABBIT ON THE MOON

Sanaya raised her arms high, joined hands over her head then gently rolled her torso to one side, keeping her lower body still. The more she stretched, the more her body tightened. Nerves were stubborn lodgers, no matter how many successful rehearsals she had under her belt with the dance troupe, or the many extra sessions with her fellow students and the dozens of solo rehearsals in her own apartment. The more her teacher and fellow dancers tried to calm her, the tighter those nerves knitted together.

It wasn't just the four hundred and twenty-three people that filled Collingwood Town Hall for the dance school showcase. Most had bought their ticket because they knew one of the dancers performing from the studio, so it was a friendly, supportive audience. The beginners had already finished their two dances and the intermediate dancers were almost at the end of their second performance. You could feel the warmth of the applause and cheering from backstage. She'd never performed publicly, like many experiences she'd been through in the last few weeks, this was new.

Loving Leo was new. Loving any man was new.

She spotted his funky brown cap in the audience during her first group performance. He said he wouldn't miss it, so that wasn't a surprise and didn't add to her edginess. Mentally and viscerally, he'd been with her every waking moment since their rain dance. This showcase ramped up in rehearsals, and he got swamped by freelance copywriting work, plus two weekends in a row with his boys, so they'd been forced into a mini break the last two weeks. But he was there all the time; memories and imaginations and funny phone calls.

"Nice stretch, Sany."

Sanaya snapped out of her Leo-land, surprised to see her leg extending a hamstring stretch at about one-hundred and twenty degrees. Frolicking in Leo-land had loosened her.

"Thanks, Mushki."

"Thinking about your boyfriend, huh?" Mushki teasing, grinning.

She tried scrunching up her face in a question and shrugged her shoulders.

"Don't act all innocent with me, your daydream smile was bigger than your stretch."

She spun away and headed for her entrance point, stage left.

Leo sensed how nervous Sanaya had been, but she needn't have worried. He was no Indian dance expert but it was obvious why the studio's head teacher had chosen her as one of the three lead dancers for the advanced students, as soon as the music started, Sanaya was in her element. She glided through the traditional Bharatnatyam tune like an eternal ghost, dancing since the creation of the ancient music. She danced deeper into his heart.

Later, in the second advanced performance, the costumes ramped up in sexiness and the pace ramped up to the title track from the huge 2008 Bollywood hit, 'Rock On!!' Sanaya radiated in a gold and purple Indian style crop-top combo.

Many in the audience took to the aisles and space in front of the stage to dance and he followed the couple he was sitting next to. Mesmerized by Sanaya on stage, and hooked on the feel good nature of the whole night, he jumped up and down and cheered with the audience when the dance finished. It took a while before Sanaya finally came out of her zone and acknowledged him. He raised his arms and bowed in a hero worship. Sanaya's smile glowed to the moon.

Just when he thought it was over, things got zanier. The opening notes of the smash hit from Slumdog Millionaire, 'Jai Ho' burst through the speakers and the whole room erupted into dancing, loud cheers and singing. Beginner and intermediary students simultaneously ran in from the sides and removed rows of connected seats from the front to enlarge the dance floor. Then they all joined in with the audience as the advanced students performed their choreographed finale. For the final couple of minutes of 'Jai Ho', the advanced dancers jumped down from the stage and joined everyone else.

❧

Sanaya beelined towards Leo. What he lacked in Bollywood technique, and that was everything, he made up for with all-in commitment and silly antics. He was obviously having a ball and she loved his uninhibited fun. When the track and final applause ended, Leo hugged Sanaya, lifted her and spun her around. When he put her back down, they held each other's hands, red scarf hanging from her wrist. She wondered what Leo was feeling about her makeup. She had painted on much more than she usually did. Checking herself in a mirror earlier, she thought it made her look a bit older. Maybe it was too much.

"You are the most beautiful woman in the world."

She was still catching her breath from the dancing, yet her heart pirouetted. She appreciated him wearing the same white shirt, blue jeans and sunset colored Indian scarf as their first date. Perfect for the event.

"You look pretty good yourself."

Leo brought his hands together in front of his chest and bowed.

"And you're amazing on stage." He had to shout to be heard above the Pussy Cat Dolls' version of 'Jai Ho' that just came on and excited the crowd all over again.

"You have to say that," Sanaya shouted.

"No. Well, yes, I do. But I really mean it. You had a huge presence up there. Like everyone else was supporting you."

"Really?" Sanaya genuinely had no idea how well she had danced. She felt the energy of the audience but only as another instrument. She knew she didn't miss a move and felt right on the rhythm the whole time, otherwise she was not conscious of her performance or how she looked.

"Yes, really. I think you'd be amazing on screen too."

"I'm not staying at your place tonight, so you can ditch the compliments."

Leo opened his mouth to say more, but instead he just stepped forward and kissed her. It became a Bollywood movie moment as some of her performance colleagues danced in a circle around them and playfully waved their scarves. Sanaya let go of Leo and tried to get out of the circle, but the crowd wouldn't let her. Leo pulled her back and kissed her again as everyone sang the chorus.

❦

"You promised to tell me the story about the rabbit on the moon," said Leo, pointing to the three-quarter moon.

Sanaya had dragged Leo away from the doting eyes and endless dancing and found a cool refuge on a bench seat in the park next to the hall.

"First, I have a confession," she said.

That sparkled Leo's eyes so she dove in quickly before his mind took off in the wrong direction.

"We studied your game, 7-Crocs, in my course at Deakin." She averted her eyes from his ego-grin. "Actually... I did a special project on you and the game. That's why I came to your talks." She wasn't ready to add that she understood now, her admiration for Leo began in that embryonic phase, before they'd even met. And that seed of admiration had blossomed into something more powerful. Something she had never expected.

It was a strange paradox because she was wading in unchartered, yet familiar waters. She was afraid to let go of those three words, *I love you*, in case she was wrong. Maybe she was over thinking it all recently. Wanting it to be more than it was. Even if she really had fallen in love with Leo, when was the right time to tell him? Shouldn't he say it first? She turned to face him.

"I think that makes you my first groupie," said Leo.

"You're impossible."

Sanaya, slapped him hard on his shoulder and got up. Leo grabbed her hand and pulled her onto his lap.

"I was just kidding. I'm sorry. You're way too classy to be a groupie."

Sanaya relaxed. Leo loosened his grip.

"My solo entourage."

She struggled to escape, but he wrapped his arms tightly around her waist.

"Would you like my autograph?"

Sanaya slapped his cheek playfully. He laughed and that softened her again.

"I really want to hear the rabbit story."

She tried a defiant glare but it was no hope, her heart bobbed up and down in the harbor of his arms and eyes. She loved his cheekiness. Their sparring was always harmless and fun. She couldn't imagine being with anyone conservative and boring. No question this guy had raised the bar.

"Please," Leo said softly.

She rested her head on Leo's shoulder, both looking at the rabbit on the moon. She hoped she could tell the story as well as her dad told it to her so many times...

"Thousands of years ago, a monkey, an otter, a jackal and a rabbit decided they would do something especially charitable on the next full moon. When that night came, an old man limped towards them begging for food. The friends knew this was their moment to really help someone in need. The monkey quickly scampered up trees and brought back berries. The otter jumped into the river and came back with a fish. The jackal, being cheeky like you," Sanaya slapped Leo's thigh and he grinned, "stole some milk from a nearby farm. The rabbit only knew how to eat grass and dig holes. Desperate to offer the man something tasty, he threw himself into the fire."

"Wow," said Leo, "is that how——"

Sanaya covered his mouth with her hand.

"The old man was actually the God, Sakra. He stopped the rabbit from reaching the fire. He was so touched by the rabbit's sacrifice, that he drew the rabbit on the moon so that the rabbit would never be forgotten."

"That's a beautiful story. Thank you." Leo kissed her cheek. "All these years I've pointed out the rabbit on the moon to people and I never knew this story."

She snuggled into Leo, wrapping her arms around his, staring at the rabbit on the moon. She wondered if that's what love was about. Throwing your heart on the fire. And if you were with the right person it didn't burn, it just glowed forever, like the rabbit on the moon.

14

GOODBYE CAFE

Leo's plane touched down yesterday, his feelings had taken another day to land.

"Ouch."

He'd bumped his arm into a door knob, third time in a few hours he'd bumped it into something. He rubbed it and wondered why these things always came in threes. It wasn't jetlag clumsiness, or exhaustion from the ten-day trip to London and Wales, something else dragged at his feet and clouded his concentration. The first symptoms felt physical but he had to accept the fear and sadness swelling inside were brewing from deep in his soul. The short time away helped to give him a clearer prism of his relationship with Sanaya.

He'd been invited to speak at a Mobile Games Conference in London. Again, he felt like an imposter on the panel, especially after he'd attended many of the other sessions. They all featured speakers who were obviously passionate about games and opportunities in the smartphone medium. The three-day conference finished with a late dinner on Friday night.

The next day he visited Travis, the son of a close friend, who had been based in London for a few years. Travis's wife, Lucy, recently gave birth to their first child, Summer. Leo had brought them gifts from Travis's dad and his own gift. Watching Lucy's pure joy and love for little Summer was a beautiful thing. When he left, his joy for them quickly drowned in melancholy. At the time, Leo put it down to sentimental memories of his own gushing when his children were born. He wasn't consciously comparing the fact that Lucy was twenty-eight years old, exactly the same age as Sanaya.

Back home, Lucy and baby Summer kept floating through Leo's mind, prompting emotions he didn't want to process. Sitting on a rock near a river bend in Templestowe, the wind made it colder than it should have been, but Leo was rugged up in a beany, red scarf and zip-up Katmandu jacket. In recent years, this is where he came to celebrate, to contemplate and sometimes, just be. He had a spiritual connection with this river, going back to when he mischievously sneaked down there as a child on his bike, against his parents' orders.

The ducks had given up on him and followed the current in hope of other easy food. The water rushed through the rocks nearby, creating mini-rapids and a hypnotic base to the natural soundtrack of birds. The tall gum trees watched over him like wise elders.

He was already grieving for the relationship he was about to end. Because it was clear to him now. He couldn't risk staying with Sanaya when any year in the next twelve she was likely to want to have children. He was already forty-eight with three healthy boys. He'd done his bit for the survival of the human species. He loved his kids dearly and was struggling to be a good dad for them, let alone have more. Not having more children was a decision he'd made even before his marriage ended. The vasectomy was an easy commitment, despite every man's hyper-sensitivity to that region of their body.

He couldn't contemplate having young children heading into his sixties. Kids suck up a lot of your energy. You don't hesitate in giving it; it's not even a conscious thing. You want to give them every ounce of your soul. He knows some men become dads at fifty but most of those didn't have any children. Others start second young families around that age. Well that was their journey, not Leo's. He'd also seen, or followed, stories about women that never imagined themselves as mothers, suddenly become obsessed with having a baby. One day they wake up with a spiritual umbilical cord tugging at their heart. Then all they can do is think about having a baby and who to have a baby with.

His romantic path had included heart-jarring baby potholes. Maria, maybe a true soul mate, was thirty-five when they broke up because she always knew she wanted kids. Erica was thirty-seven, living a fiercely independent lifestyle and never dreamed of being a mom until she fell in love with Leo and spent time with his kids.

Kali was forty-three years old when she ended their

engagement because she wanted her own little girl. Forty-three! Then she followed her biological clock down the rocky IVF road on her own for twelve months before finally accepting her seedless fate. He felt for all of them and would never stand in their way. He genuinely hoped they would achieve their motherly need. But it was always with a battered heart.

He loved Sanaya. And she loved him too, despite her consistent aloofness to anything remotely romantic. That's why he had to end it. However painful the break up was now, it would be unbearable in five to ten years. She deserved the opportunity to experience the indescribable joy of becoming a mother. She was much too young to slam that door shut now. Besides, you can't shut that door. When Mother-Evolution starts ticking, she finds her way through the most stubborn and protected doors, gates and walls.

Some relationships were easy-ish to walk away from. But even when both people agree that it's the right thing to do, it's never really easy. There's always stuff to work through and let go. Walking away from someone you deeply love, and who loves you, is hard.

Better to do it before they both gave birth to those powerful three words "I love you".

Because three words plus three words don't add up to six. They add up to millions of shared words and bonding moments. Thousands of sticky tentacles and fibers that interweave your lives. Once those six words are released into the world, unravelling them is complex. They exacerbate the pain. It didn't matter that they had been together just five months. The intensity of their connection was obvious.

Leo didn't want to be the messenger on this one. He was struggling to accept the message himself; to walk away from Sunface and her pure joy. But it had to be him, had to be face to face. So, he peeled himself off the cold rock and walked home to shower and change before meeting with Sanaya.

Sanaya had been surprised at how much she missed Leo. *How can someone glide into your life and feel like they've always been there? Like everything before evolved as a pre-life, and now that stage has served its purpose, and her future is life with Leo.*

She got to the cafe for their 'catching up' date early. It was good of him to let her choose the venue; Leo had respected her desire to not always be at his place. And today, after a couple of drinks she would invite him up the road to her apartment for the first time. Another thing Leo hadn't pushed or questioned. She'd already prepared a simple dinner and trusted him totally.

Luckily, her favorite black couch in the corner was free and she plonked herself on the window side, unable to rein in her imagination on how the rest of the day would flow. She had finally embraced this transformation in herself. When they met she genuinely had a *"whatever"* attitude to Leo and romance. She enjoyed the moments with him but that's as far as she was, in the moment.

Now she couldn't stop thinking about things they could do together. She had plans for showing off her favorite parts of India, parading him to Mushki and Ajala and all her other cousins and Mumbai friends. The many parts of the world they could discover together. At first, she thought it was just his absence in the UK that might have been messing with her. But, eventually, she had to own up. She was in love with Leo.

Leo had breezed past the fences and high gates protecting her, knocked on the front door, waltzed into her heart and made himself at home. Now her skin tingled just waiting to see him. To give him the gift she prepared. To soak in his eyes when she told him her other surprise - the perfect way to tell him how she felt. He would love her gesture, something creative and romantic that she would never have imagined doing a few months ago.

She loved this tiny space, in a less than trendy pocket of Hawthorn, but it had a warmth. The two guys who ran it in their Bob Marley hair, colorful t-shirts and harem pants, were a walking atmosphere. Marley's "Could You Be Loved" filtered gently out of the speakers.

That has to be a sign! Oh, girl, how much you've changed. It's my time. Yes, I can be loved.

Goodbye Cafe.

Leo's nickname for the venue about to host their saddest date. Black humor often helped him cope in these moments. No love theme playing from Slumdog Millionaire today.

Goodbye Cafe. It could be a successful franchise.

He wondered about the number of sad endings he'd endured at all the 'Goodbye Cafes' around Melbourne. Four, maybe five times. A franchise like that would help prepare the unsuspecting partner for the bad news coming, take the edge off the final delivery. *"See you at Goodbye Cafe."* Big hint. That's ninety percent of the hard work done in advance.

A neutral venue was always best. Somewhere either one of you could walk away from. *Always know your escape route...* that's what De Niro's character had said in some action thriller a few years ago. Leo had made the mistake of ending one of his relationships at his home and that created an awkward scenario when the woman controlled the physical act of leaving. And she didn't want to leave.

Leo's silly internal banter vanished with the thump of his car door closing. He took a deep breath and walked towards the cafe carrying his small goodbye gift.

⚜

"It's beautiful," said Sanaya, holding the notebook Leo had bought for her in London. She caressed the embossed apple-tree pattern on the red leather cover then flipped it open to reveal thick blank pages, a little bigger than the throwaway notebook she usually dragged around, but small enough to fit in her handbag.

"This is a bit freaky because I have something for

you too." She pulled out her own gift and handed it to him.

He held it and stared at what felt like a DVD. He knew he had to open the gift, but after that, he promised himself, no more procrastination on his Goodbye Cafe mission. After slowly unwrapping the paper, he could see it was a thin DVD cover but he couldn't open it to check out the contents because he was struck by the cover; a pencil drawing of the location of their first meeting on Platform 9. Sanaya must have got the street illustrator who based himself outside Flinders Street station to do it.

"Can you see it?"

He noticed the red apple sitting on the bench near where they met. Amongst the all grey drawing of the empty platform, the small red apple was so obvious once you saw it. Symbolizing her Facebook photo and the first poem he sent her, 'Apple Smile'. His heart sank deep into his stomach. *She gives me such a loving, romantic gift today, of all days.* He avoided Sanaya's eyes and opened the cover, revealing a CD.

"It's a mix-tape. Some we've heard together and some are my favorite Indian songs." Each word zinging with love, splattering his heart with guilt. "And, I've got another surprise for you."

"Sanaya, the drawing is beautiful. A really lovely surprise... and so is the music but...

I have something I need to tell you."

"Okay, you first," said Sanaya, smiling, beaming.

Leo put the CD next to her notebook on the coffee table. He could tell that she had not sensed the train coming from the other end of the heart-shaped tunnel she was skipping through. The irony was almost as painful as what he was about to do. It took him five months to help her move from romantic apathy to romantic. And now he had to crush that. Hopefully, for her soul it would only be a temporary scar.

"We have to end our relationship."

Sanaya's entire body stilled. Her eyes giant question marks.

"What do you mean?"

"I want to be with you, but I can't."

"Why?"

Leo could feel the icicles in her one word response.

She straightened her back, incessantly dancing hands stilled on her knees. "Did you meet someone else while you were away?"

"No, no. I haven't met anyone and right now can't imagine being with someone else." He straightened and held her hands. "At some stage you might want to have children. And I don't."

"I don't want to have children."

"You say that now, but you're only twenty-eight. You can't tell me right now how you're going to feel about that in two years' time, or seven years, or when you get close to forty."

"Neither can you."

He nodded gently, "I don't know for sure. I just know the odds are high, the risk of breaking our hearts too high."

"Now is all we know. You said that; one of the wisest

things I've ever heard. We can't predict the future, now *IS* all we know."

He usually hated when his own words were thrown back at him, yet he could only admire the clarity amongst her shock.

"I thought this was special. We have a connection that's bigger than our age difference," said Sanaya.

"We do and that's why this is so hard. But if you do want children, and we have to end our relationship in ten years' time, I'll be nearly sixty." Leo felt ninety with the weight of the words and the sadness in Sanaya's eyes.

She reached for her Chinotto but didn't pick it up. A million thoughts must've been swirling inside the poor thing, battling to flood out but none of them knew how to make sense of what he'd dumped on her.

"You don't know how I'll feel in ten years."

"That's the risk I'm taking today. But I've seen women that never dreamed of having children, then it hits them and it's all they can think about."

"I thought you loved me." Part statement, part plea.

He had to answer without digging them deeper, yet honor their love. He swirled the remaining ice in his glass with the straw. Sanaya uncurled her leg that was bent on the couch and placed both feet on the floor. Her fingers were crisscrossed on her lap and her thumbs pressed back and forth on each other.

"I might be making the biggest mistake of my life. I don't think I'll ever find anyone like you."

"You don't have to, I'm right here."

"Sanaya..."

"Don't worry about your vasectomy, we can always adopt."

And there it was.

In her dazed state, as her heart was shriveling into dust, her own soul couldn't actually slide the door closed on becoming a mother. He found some relief from the mutual torture he was putting them through. But that was only relative relief. Even the ice in his glass had given up the fight and dissolved into murkiness. He looked at Sanaya's half-filled glass.

"You said you had another surprise. Was it throwing your drink at me?"

Somehow a smile worked its way through to Sanaya's mouth, but her eyes were filled with sadness.

"I booked a love song dedication for you on Sun-FM." She stared at him.

Poisoned irony.

He'd always craved someone to dedicate a song to him on that show. His stomach wrapped up his heart, fell to the floor, and rolled outside into the gutter.

A part of him wished he had delayed this decision so they could have celebrated her courageous romantic gesture.

"Wow, Sanaya, when?"

"Tomorrow night," she said without looking up, "I'll have to call them now and change the story."

What she had planned as a beautiful surprise had become a blunt weapon. But the blow clobbered them both. His ego and curiosity teamed up to push through the torture.

"What song?"

Sanaya faced him, tears in her eyes.

"You'll have to listen." Her voice croaky, last word barely letting go of her tongue.

He nodded. There wasn't going to be a quick release from their agony. As he studied Sanaya's cheerless, almost lifeless eyes, he realized he had inflicted her first romantic scar. It was not a 'first' to celebrate. Instinctively he kissed the fingers on his right hand and gently placed them over Sanaya's heart. He was thankful for the almost imperceptible smile through her tears.

She kissed his palm, then held it on her cold, drained cheek. After a few seconds, she snuggled into his shoulder and they lay back into the couch.

Despite their empty glasses, the Reggae Twins sensed this was a delicate corner of the world that they should not disturb. One of them turned the music down as Jimmy Cliff sang "*I can see clearly now the rain has gone*". While the lyric was counter to the mood, the melody and rhythm soothed. He stroked Sanaya's hair as they watched the world blur past outside. Neither of them was in a hurry to end their final intimate moment together, as Sanaya's raw virgin scar and his torturous dilemma searched for a way to become friends.

❧ 15 ❧

LIGHT IN YOUR STAR

Sanaya had enjoyed being an only child. Enjoyed the space of living alone as an adult, even in a tiny apartment in a foreign city. Sculpting her solo life physically and emotionally in Melbourne was the natural expression of her spirit.

She'd read books and heard from others how everything seemed more cavernous when a serious relationship ended. A vast emptiness.

Then why am I suffocating?

Everywhere she scanned around her apartment, memories of Leo smothered her. The lantern he'd bought during the Diwali Festival of Lights celebration. The framed Slumdog Millionaire poster from him on her bedroom wall. The blank TV screen beamed back visions of moments together. Whenever it rained, their crazy rain dance in his backyard drenched her in melancholy. The number of romantic couples on the streets had suddenly multiplied by a million. EVERY song on her playlists tortured.

She couldn't breathe without choking on Leo.

Sanaya stared at the large cushion in her lap. She'd picked apart the first four letters of embroidery from her mom; *Raajakumaaree* was now *akumaaree.* No longer a full Princess, just a meaningless bunch of letters.

Perfect.

She pushed the cushion onto the couch and sought solace from her little Lakshmi statute. Lakshmi's four hands only confused her. She needed just one finger pointing her in the right direction. Was she naïve in this century expecting to remain a virgin till marriage? Where did that commitment come from anyway? Not her mother, not even her dad. A stupid declaration she'd secretly made with Ajala on her 16th birthday and a stubbornness to not foresee the impact it had on her love life. Her heart.

Ajala's recent revelation had initially stunned then annoyed her. How could her cousin not be brave enough to stick to their mutual virgin vows? Then she realized Ajala was braver, living *her* life on *her* terms in a community conflicted between insular ancient rituals in an open modern world.

Maybe Sanaya's virgin vows had helped her avoid a few painful misjudgments but she believed in Leo's love. She had needed to know Leo loved her forever without sex, before she was willing to explore their passion. In the safety of Leo, her virgin vows seemed irrelevant. All it did was deprive her of a beautiful dimension to an amazing relationship. Surely, if that ancient obstacle didn't exist in her life, Leo still would.

Or would he? Leo had also released an emotional

worm into her consciousness, like a computer virus it worked its way through her mind and heart, with one foreign piece of programming. Baby. Mother. Raising a child. Yet the flickers of a future nurturing a child, were drowned out by her monsoon of despair. She missed Leo.

They'd been apart longer than five days before, but there was always a next time, plus some form of communication. He hadn't contacted her since the café catastrophe. No reaction to her love song dedication on the radio. The most original romantic act of her life turned into an audio shower of shame. When she'd rung the show's producer to cancel the dedication, the poor guy ended up hearing her sad story and tears, then she changed her mind clinging to the hope Leo would realize his mistake after her open-heart-radio-surgery.

Nothing.

Leo had also been a ghost on social media, ignoring her 'likes' on old photos of him, of them. She had to break through his stubborn stupidity. Embarrassment would be a kinder pain than the hell in her heart.

She picked up her phone. Scrolled to his number. Again. Stared at it, again. Then scrolled up to Ajala's number. In a moment of weakness, she'd messaged Ajala her break-up news the night it happened, and her cousin had called immediately, but Sanaya didn't take or return the call, determined to deal with her own pain, while still disappointed with Ajala secretly breaking their secret vows.

"Namaste bhavy." Ajala's husky energy wrapped her in a vocal hug.

Sanaya didn't even realize she'd hit the 'call' button and certainly didn't feel anything remotely gorgeous. She burst out in sloppy, raw sobs that rocked her body from the waist up. She dropped the phone on the couch and covered her face with her hands, trying to steady her head, her neck. Seemed to take hours before she settled, elbows on knees, head heavy on her hands. A distant mantra whispered *"It's okay Sany, tears bathe your soul… It's okay Sany, tears bathe your soul… It's okay Sany, tears bathe your soul…"*

It was Ajala on the phone. She wiped her eyes with her sleeves and picked up the phone.

"Sorry, Aju, so embarrassing."

"Do not apologize for sharing your soul with me. Ever."

"When I'm not drowning in pain I'm spinning with confusion."

"You're human and you loved him and—"

"And, I want a baby."

"Oh, Sany, can't you see, that's why Leo blessed your life, to awaken your deepest yearning. Such a beautiful thing," said Ajala.

"Then why is my heart like a funeral?"

"Mourn your time with Leo, that is, natural, healthy, but never be sad that you want a baby."

"This is torture Aju. I want a baby *with* Leo. There is no clear path."

"Sanaya Gupta, you are my Piku, my Queen Rani. Whenever I am stuck in the mud of life, I think, 'What would Sany do?' You have so much light Sany, I borrow from your life-storch all the time to show me the way forward."

She'd never imagined being compared to their movie heroines, Rani and Piku, let alone by Ajala, the fiercest woman she knew. The fog clouding her mind still clung to her thoughts but the weight in her tummy and heart lifted.

"I love you Aju."

"I love you too bhavy. Trust your own light and I'm here whenever you need."

Sanaya teared up again but this time with tears of love.

"Thanks, ciao." She hung up and smiled despite the tears. She'd said 'ciao', Leo's favorite sign-off. How did he infuse so much into her in such a short time? She stared at Lakshmi, "Where is my light, favorite Goddess, which way is it shining?"

She wiped her eyes, sat back and crossed her legs on the couch. Ajala was right. If she could create a life away from her parents and birth country, she could do anything. She closed her eyes and rested her hands on her thighs, thumb and finger in a circle. Meditation wasn't her regular door to clarity in complex situations, usually dancing or yoga did the trick. But this problem needed something deeper. She focused on her breathing, feeling it flow through her nostrils. With each breath she felt it deeper, flowing down her throat, then lungs.

Poetry.

The words blazed into her eyelids.

Poetry lubricated the beginning of their relationship,

maybe poetry could resurrect it. She opened her eyes, pulled her mom's cushion back onto her lap, picked up her laptop from the side table and rested it on the cushion.

❧

The love-song dedication that Leo had secretly been craving turned out to be Taylor Swift's 'Love Story'. While it was the saddest musical moment of his life, it must have been worse for Sanaya. Devastatingly worse. He didn't record it but would never forget the hollow echo in his heart as he heard Sanaya explain her selection to the announcer.

"He is the only guy that ever called me a Princess and he made me feel like one. And now I have my own love story. Even though it's a sad one." Her voice breaking as she mumbled the final few words.

The announcer gave her a verbal hug and it was all over in what felt like seconds.

He resisted thanking Sanaya or contacting her at all. Previous heartbreaks taught him he couldn't be the person to help Sanaya get over him. He understood her yearning for *"one more meeting"*. He'd often pleaded for the same thing in the past; that aching need to try and make sense of a sudden ending you never saw coming, and maybe, if you were in the same space again, the original magic would return and reverse the train wreck. Take both of you back to a time when you were sitting in the same carriage, holding hands and heading in the same direction. Somewhere in the future, there could be a way for them to be friends, but the early journey to closure wasn't the time.

Ignoring Sanaya's text messages and not responding to her Facebook notes during the first three weeks wasn't easy. Especially after their prolific creative writings throughout the five months together; sent back and forth with 'digital doves'. However, he found it impossible to ignore her email with the subject heading "Disclaimer":

It's only with you that I can share
For anyone else will not really care,
Or understand its true essence,
It'll simply fail to make any sense.
My present to you was about our past,
What I write now is the present, perhaps the very last.

His body tensed up as he clicked on the attached poem...

Apple and Moon
How do autumn tears fry?
Sharp pain under a dull sky
Yet my heart wants to at least try
To understand by asking why?
My own mind is beyond its means
Shriveled brown soul like leaves once green
Punish myself with recent scenes
Can our murky love story come clean?
Was this Latika that naïve?
Seeing a shiny Jamal she needed to believe
Is it love's trick to occasionally deceive?

Can new words from you help relieve?
This apple spun around your moon
Your gravity died much too soon.
Can we crawl back into our cocoon?
Or is my heart forever marooned?

His gentle tears dried up by the fifth reading. Sharing her raw emotions so poetically just made it harder for him to accept his decision to end it. In fact, this poem only seemed to entrench his love for her deeper. He desperately hoped Sanaya's first romantic scar did not become a seed that grew to hate him. Yes, some of that was motivated by selfish thoughts. But he knew that such hate usually hooked up with fear of loving again, and together hate and fear were incompatible romantic partners that poisoned potential relationships.

As difficult as it was letting go, he truly hoped Sanaya would find the love she deserved in all its layers and dimensions – including having children if that's where her soul took her. Friends kept telling Leo he did the noble thing. Noble wasn't easy. Of all the relationships that Leo has had to walk away from, Sanaya is the only woman whose footsteps he occasionally felt strolling through his heart. Leo wasn't wise enough to know how things would work out for Sanaya, or whether he would find someone again that touched him the way she did.

He learned something valuable from every relationship, even those that left the deepest scars. They pushed him to become wiser and more aware of himself and, therefore, more open to the feelings and needs of others. Scars can become cavernous ditches, or part of the sagacious map that guides your heart. In the end, you own that choice.

He didn't want more children; this was meant to be his time. He'd committed to live close to the boys and be as involved as he possibly could in their lives until Joey turned eighteen. Then he might base himself in New York or Paris for a while, or be a gypsy in Spain and Italy. He didn't regret any personal sacrifice that was a consequence of being their dad. Sacrifice wasn't even the right word, they brought so much joy into his life and helped him become a better person.

'Hey, Dad', was the sweetest sound in his life. He couldn't imagine his life without James, Thomas and Joey. He couldn't imagine becoming a father again. He'd already suffered from three relationships that ended because the women wanted children. He was inching towards fifty. Would he ever connect with a woman like Sanaya again? Was he an 'idiota' walking away from her on the hope that he might? They could have possibly ten amazing years before Sanaya was sure she wanted children. He could stumble through ten years of dating other women without connecting with a spirit like Sanaya.

But how many years could he be with her without making love? Sanaya's virgin vow versus their raw passion. He believed in love, in marriage, in finding his soulmate. That meant meeting a partner on mutual paths. Having another child was not his path. Rushing marriage just to consummate a loving, adult relationship was not a healthy path.

Sanaya was not his forever path.

His stomach and heart remained wound up tight since Goodbye Café. His thoughts stalked Sanaya through their time together. This decision was the most excruciating since leaving his wife. He cancelled paid games seminar appearances. Missed marketing deadlines that would help 7-Crocs in new territories. Couldn't even write a speculative article to magazine editor that had invited a submission. The only inspiration came from his goodbye-muse, Sanaya. Her poem broke the dam wall holding his words. He hit reply on her email and typed.

> *As your star continues to grow*
> *Reflect on some of the people you know*
> *They help make us who we are*
> *Even those that left a scar.*
> *You deserve to enjoy the glow*
> *Don't let it burn your sweet soul*
> *Share the light high and far*
> *The special light in your star.*

He lifted his feet onto the porch timber rail, picked up his gin and tonic and swirled the glass as he reread the poem. Every now and then, very rarely, his words felt like they'd been written by someone much wiser and more talented. The poem had rattled out of him complete. Hopefully, it will help both of them edge towards the road of closure. How quickly they could move down the road and when they would reach Closure-Town, he wasn't wise enough to know. Closure doesn't come with signs or a schedule. No social media notifications claiming "Congratulations, your heart is cured you can move on now!"

He hit send, put his laptop on the upside down plastic crate he used as a table, leaned back and stared at the clouds. An article he'd read about the Japanese philosophy, Wabi Sabi drifted into his thoughts. Despite being wary about a westerner interpreting ancient eastern beliefs, the simple summary had stuck. Nothing is permanent, nothing ends, nothing is perfect.

Sanaya was the almost perfect partner.

Her impact would never end.

Their relationship never had a chance at being permanent.

❦ 16 ❦

EIGHTEEN MONTHS LATER

After dating three guys that summer, Sanaya had given up on the idea of a second date. Given up on her ability to judge dudes. Finding duds she was good at. Exceptional dud-finding skills. Decent dudes, fail.

Until Zafar.

Zafar kept her from retreating back into the solo life she'd committed to post-Leo. Zafar was the first guy to make her laugh uncontrollably since that old dude with the three kids and a vasectomy. He'd helped her slip into a stage where she could think about Leo without her tummy tightening. Without spiraling into a million *what-ifs*. Zafar's smile made him look taller than his average physique, but she rarely wore heels so they were ok. Sweeter than mom's chai; she'd love Zafar. And the dude had a good soul; a nurse who chose to work in aged care. The kind of caregiver she'd wish for her parents in the future.

But he couldn't dance to save starving children. Even

his joyful smile couldn't cover that up. Which was ok. He'd surprised her by suggesting to go to the St Kilda Festival for date three. On Valentine's Day. Any other date suggestion on look-at-me-I'm-so-romantic-Valentine's Day would have been a no-go for her. But she loved the energy of the St Kilda Festival and was lost in The Bamboos' funky music when the threatening dark clouds launched a thunder storm. The band had to stop and take cover. By the time an official announced the concert would be delayed until the storm had ended, most of the crowd had already scattered.

Scurrying across slippery grass in Catani Gardens towards Zafar's car, she heard The Bamboos', 'On The Sly' boom out of speakers and stopped to see if the band was risking it back on stage. The music was coming from a gazebo packed with a dozen or more people and a DJ sound system that must've already been set up there.

Plus, at least a hundred crazy folk dancing around the gazebo in the heavy rain.

"Come on Sany, we're almost there," yelled Zafar, holding a knapsack with their water bottles and snacks over his head, pointing to his car with the other hand.

Her body was already swaying to the beat. A deep force dragged her to the rain party.

"I'm gonna dance."

"You're crazy."

"Yes." She swayed backwards to the gazebo. "Come with me." It was impossible get any more soaked and it wasn't cold.

"I'll put this in the car first."

"Okay." And she spun towards the gazebo.

Closer to the crowd, the Bamboos' rhythm blended with the percussion of the rain bouncing off the gazebo's iron roof. Groups danced in circles, arms around shoulders. Couples found their own groove. Sanaya closed her eyes and slipped into a solo zone, deep into her soul where music always took her.

Laughter snuck through her dance-trance. A couple on their knees, swaying arms in harmony and laughing. Raw. Uninhibited. Joy. The vision catapulted her back to Leo's backyard. Her veins simmered, her heart beat louder than the rain. Louder than the music blasting from the speakers. Like it was yesterday. With Leo.

"Sany, Sany."

She turned and there was Zafar at the edge of the dancing throng, holding a huge umbrella, a blanket around his shoulders.

She glanced at the couple, who weren't laughing anymore because they were passionately kissing. Still on their knees, oblivious to the hundreds of people dancing around them, oblivious to the torrential rain. Lost in each other.

She looked back at Zafar. He waved an arm from under the blanket for her to join him, unable to move closer through the crowd without closing his ridiculous umbrella.

Sanaya closed her eyes.

"All done. Just rest there a moment and I'll be back to make sure there's no seepage."

Sanaya opened her eyes just as the doctor escaped through the corner of the privacy curtains around her emergency ward bed. She studied the white bandage on her right hip. No pain from the wound or the stitches but that's only because of the local anesthetic. Luckily it was towards the softer buttock area rather than hip bone. The doctor said that would have been trickier with healing, and more painful.

What a bevakooph.

Poor Zafar. Sweet, sometimes funny, safe Zafar.

He hadn't put a foot wrong in their five almost completed dates. Not a stray hand either. Zafar didn't have any edges, just one safety zone after another. He'd be a perfect husband for someone, but not her. The moment she saw him under the umbrella it was over. The rain dance in Catani Gardens washed away all the sandbags she'd been stacking around her heart; the heavens poured down on Melbourne and Leo flooded back in. Zafar could never match Leo's lingering love.

She'd scurried through the dancing crowd, away from Zafar, found the beachside path and struggled against the southerly wind, head down from the angled rain. No point taking shelter because it wouldn't have stopped the monsoon in her mind.

She loved Leo. Missed him deeply.

He'd lit a star in her universe that dulled every other man on the planet.

Damn Leo. He's the bevakooph for walking away from me!

He ended it just as she was accepting it. He didn't

think her worthy enough to reconsider having another child. He dumped her just before the public commitment of her love on radio. His presence taunted her on Facebook. Months of nothing, then a 'congratulations' note when she posted her first serious job at Portable Research. AND the owners turned out to be friends of his. She loved the gig, enjoyed the challenge of coming up with games-oriented activities for elderly people suffering cognitive issues such as dementia, but nearly resigned wondering if he'd helped behind the scenes. He promised he hadn't. Then no communication since.

She was getting back into the groove of her perfect universe: only child, solo adult, happy heart. Dating a nice guy. Until one stupid rain dance and she's running like a madwoman in a wild storm.

She had stepped on something and her right foot slipped. She'd braced her fall a little with her hands on the top of the short stonewall but her hip bore the brunt of the landing. And all the agony. Sobbing, drenched, maimed. Luckily a couple driving past saw her fall. They pulled over, helped her compose herself and insisted on driving her to the Alfred hospital. The sweet woman wouldn't leave until Sanaya had been admitted into the ER ward. Apparently she'd stepped on a Frisbee. Probably dropped by someone as they rushed to their car when the storm unleashed.

The abrasions on her hands and right elbow would heal first, then her hip. That left a Leo scar she couldn't suture, couldn't cover with a bandage. A clear sign she had to make a final emotional break; if it wasn't for him, she'd never have been on that stupid path in driving rain in a cloud of Leo musings. Even if they tried again, could she trust him to commit? She'd moved on from her virgin vows and could imagine Leo's wavy hair on the pillow next to hers. But was that enough? She couldn't stand going through the torture of breaking up with him a second time.

The storm had brought rain dancing and that seemed to bring back Leo. But it was clear now, everything had happened to wash Leo away.

"Knock, knock." Dr Tatarka slipped back in through the curtains. "Feeling ok?"

Sanaya made a final decision. A move-on mission-decision that had no time for wallowing in scars or blaming Leo. He was absolutely the past.

"Yes."

The doctor pulled over the plastic chair and examined her hip. "No seepage that's good but you're going to have to minimize movement for a few days. The stitches should dissolve in a week. That's the sign when you can step up mobility." She sat back and smiled, her long auburn curls in a ponytail settled over the left of her neck. "I've already told you about showering, any other questions?"

"Will it leave a scar?"

"Your hands and elbow will heal fully. Your hip might leave a war wound. Lucky for you, only your most intimate friend will get to see it." She winked and grinned.

No intimate friend was going to see her scar.

"That's some war face, Sanaya. Sorry, I didn't mean to assume anything."

"Will it heal quicker if I take the bandage off and let the wound air?"

"No, that's a myth, keep the bandage on." said Dr Tatarka. She leaned forward, studied Sanaya. "Wounds heal from the inside."

"Inside?" Sanaya wasn't sure what the doctor meant.

"The skin cells inside your body mend and gel first, then the outer skin."

She'd always imagined it the other way around, that you needed something external, like air and ointment.

"A scar may stay with you forever, but it has no purpose once it heals. It can remind you of pain, or it can remind you how tough you are. That's up to you." Dr Tatarka removed her latex gloves and squeezed her hand, more mother-like than medical, "The key thing to accept is all scars heal from the inside."

✦

Two days later she called Zafar and explained as gently as she could, she didn't want to continue dating. She preferred to do it in person, but her injuries needed rest and Zafar deserved to know. The poor dude had texted her and left voicemail messages since she'd run off at the festival. She didn't dare tell him about her accident because he would've driven straight over insisting to take care of her.

They had only known each other just over a month. And still the 'this isn't going to work out' call was hard.

Zafar's shock reverberated with questions. Why, what had he done, what could he do? His sweetness right to the final goodbye made it more excruciating. After ending the call, her hands trembled, tears dribbled down her cheek. She empathized deeply with Zafar as the experience had triggered the scarring end inflicted upon her by Leo.

Sitting on the bed with legs straight, back leaning on pillows, she flattened her hands on her thighs, closed her eyes and breathed slowly. Dr Tatarka's words floated into her thoughts. *A scar may stay with you forever, but it has no purpose once it heals. It can remind you of pain, or it can remind you how tough you are… The key thing to accept is all scars heal from the inside.*

She had healed from Leo and now it was time to appreciate the good from their time together and stop picking at the emotional scar. Actually, her call to Zafar highlighted the kindness and courage Leo had shown by ending their relationship in person. She'd heard pathetic stories of guys and women ending relationships by text, or worse, via social media. Leo had been honest and gentle and caring. She was more comfortable with her own romanticism thanks to Leo. She'd always been independent, but now there was a confident calmness rather than bravado at its foundation.

She would date again. Not aggressively pursue romance, but also not resist it. In fact, she would embrace it.

Some lucky dude was going to fall in love with an amazing woman.

Sanaya Gupta!

17

FESTIVAL OF RAIN

"Why not?" said Caroline, tone and grin dripping with mischief.

Leo had suggested they share dessert and her response could not have been more steamy, head on an angle, deep green eyes sparkling, blonde locks laying on tanned cleavage. He'd almost not followed up after the first date. They'd been introduced by mutual friends which had created an additional layer of tension. Fortunately, they gave it a second chance and everything about the evening whispered sexual fun; starting with her red mini dress, to one of his secret sensual pleasures, sharing dessert.

The waiter caught Leo's gaze and hovered over.

"We'll have the Chocolate Blood, please." His mouth watered just ordering the chocolate cake with raspberry sauce.

"With two scoops of ice-cream," said Caroline.

A nice surprise based on her unfinished chicken

salad. Funny, sexy and sharing two scoops of ice-cream with dessert. He liked Caroline.

"What coffee would you like?" asked the very Melbourne waiter.

"No coffee, two Bellini's please," said Caroline.

Leo's face must've given away he was no cocktail connoisseur.

"Champagne with peach schnapps. It will give the dessert an extra sizzle," she said.

"Sizzle away!"

She sizzled him out of his comfort zone and that didn't happen often. It was going to be an amazing night.

"Excellent choice," said the waiter. He turned to leave.

"And we need the cake cut onto two separate plates, one ice-cream scoop each, and separate cutlery of course," said Caroline.

The waiter nodded.

Leo's gut morphed from hungry to heavy. That wasn't sharing, it was one dessert cut up as two separate serves. A clear demarcation. As sensual as McDonald's drive-thru. Like booking a hotel for a honeymoon with two separate single beds.

❧

The sex was good. Guilt-free. He'd taken six months to honor his love for Sanaya. Took another twelve months of going-through-the-motions of sexual hook-ups before Caroline sizzled through his defenses. So the sex was good. Caroline didn't want him to stay the whole night and he happily slipped out of her trendy apartment.

Back home, he'd grabbed a can of Chinotto from his fridge, shuffled onto the back porch and plonked onto the picnic chair, feet resting on the lower timber rail. Neither early morning, nor dawn; the only sound came from bats as they raided his neighbor's giant plum tree. Little squeaks. Shadows of movement. A reflection of his heart since dessert. Squeaking questions. Answers lurking in the shadows. Circling one subject.

Sanaya.

What if she never wanted children? He would've thrown away the best relationship with the most fascinating woman for nothing. Worst case: if she really wanted a child and left him, they could've enjoyed five to ten fun, blissful years together. Where's the harm in that? What are the chances of meeting someone else he'd connect with so deeply, seamlessly? He'd already had more than his fair share of the romance universe. How much luck could one guy attract on this planet? He'd pushed away Sanaya for what? Selfishness? Fear? Ego?

Stars studied him, then the moon emerged from behind clouds. He smiled, reminiscing at Sanaya's 'rabbit on the moon' story. Was he willing to sacrifice his goals, his preconceived future into the blazing fire of Sanaya's heart? Isn't that what he always believed about love? Committing one hundred percent to someone you love? He'd had clear plans about his creative career and look how that had played out. His goal of writing magazine articles around quirky people and east-versus-west lifestyle pieces, took a depressing detour into mobile games, which led to meeting Nick Blades at a digital media seminar in Cannes, which led to his new gig of creating video stories for *Blades Babel*, the fastest growing lifestyle online magazine.

Writing and directing videos didn't just fulfil his creative ambition, it added layers and challenges he enjoyed. None of which he could've predicted. The future isn't a map; it's a maze with hidden exits into opportunities your brain hasn't invented yet. So why was he so stubborn about who he was supposed to fall in love with…and when? Two absolutes he'd learned on Romantic Road, nothing is more unpredictable than the heart, and opportunities for love are rare.

Clouds covered the moon again. He scratched his arm then lower leg, flapped at a mosquito buzzing near his ear. Exhaustion overcame him; he crushed the empty Chinotto can and headed inside.

❧

"Do you always celebrate the Holi Festival together?" said Leo.

Mother and daughter stared at each other for a few seconds then burst out laughing.

The camera Simon had set-up with a mid-shot of both of them would capture the twin-joy. Out of the corner of his eye, he sensed Simon panning the other camera, with the super close-up, from mother to daughter. The women were drenched with water and the glorious hues of the festival colors; splashes of purple, yellow, orange, green, pink and red.

They didn't call the Holi Festival the festival of colors by accident and he was grateful *Blades Babel* had agreed to let him do a mini-documentary video. If you couldn't travel the world creating stories, then Melbourne was the place to be. The world came to you with endless multicultural festivals and events.

"Actually, this is the first time we've come here together since Preeti turned seventeen," said Myra, focused on her daughter. "We had a big fight because after two years of studying accounting, Preeti changed her university degree to fashion design at RMIT."

"And as you probably know, the Holi Festival is all about forgiveness," said Preeti, winking at the camera.

"New starts," said Myra nodding.

They wrapped an arm around each other. He let Simon's camera soak in the emotional moment for a few seconds. It had been a fun, flowing interview and he was going to wrap it there, but his instincts pushed him to ask an unplanned question.

"Did you design what you're wearing?" Leo asked Preeti.

"She did. Isn't it beautiful?" said Myra beaming at her daughter with pride.

The power of forgiveness. Tears trickled down Myra's cheek, Preeti pulled a clean scarf from her bag and wiped them. Gold.

"Cut," said Leo. "Danny?"

Danny looked up from his sound gear and winked. Sound is the underestimated element of screen content, especially recording clear interviews with the mayhem and party music of the festival in the background. Danny was a master and Simon not only a good cameraman, he was the fastest editor in Melbourne… and patient with Leo's lack of technical language. But Leo quickly discovered that his story instincts and imagination loved playing in the medium. He would come up with ideas that added emotional depth to the video and Simon could make them work within minutes. He knew this video was one of the most visual and entertaining they'd shot and couldn't wait to get into the post-production process with Simon.

"Thank you so much Myra and Preeti, your honesty was beautiful and you both look amazing. You can check out the video on *Blades Babel* next Friday."

Danny took the lapel mics from the women who then headed for the safety of food and drink vans on the perimeter of the wild dancing. Hundreds had honored the official speeches at Fed Square and now, just down the river at The Paddock, thousands partied to music in the unique, giant pit of a venue. People threw clouds of colorful powder in the air and water balloons at each other. The combination created a spectacular visual feast with everyone splattered in a hues of purple, pink, orange, red and lime. By the time he turned back to ask Simon if he wanted to shoot more of the party, he'd already grabbed his gimbal and somehow talked his way past the security guy and onto the DJ stage. Danny had packed up his stuff and hovered protectively over Simon's other camera gear.

SPLASH.

Someone had hit Leo with a water balloon, the back of his t-shirt and hair instantly soaked. Danny exploded in laughter. Leo didn't turn around, safer to ignore the source, otherwise he may end up with paint all over him next and he hadn't prepared his car for that mess. He walked towards Danny who pretended to duck.

Splash. This water balloon only caught his right shoulder, but it wet his hair and face. Danny bobbed with laughter. Leo turned this time, annoyed at the soaking, ready to give the thrower a verbal spray.

Sanaya.

Soaked in all the colors of the festival from top to toe, but he recognized her smile in a nanosecond.

Sanaya.

He'd resisted joining the dancing and human coloring, yet now the party was raging in his gut, his heart.

Whoosh, whoosh, whoosh. Three soft hits on his body.

Leo instinctively covered his face. When he opened his eyes he was covered in pink, purple and yellow. Three guys hi-fived near him.

One of them yelled out, "Jai ho, bro. Jai ho."

Sanaya laughed harder than Danny.

Sanaya, a walking festival of colors. Laughing at him.

And all he could do was laugh.

18

FESTIVAL OF COLORS

"Who taught you how to throw like that?" said Leo

"Playing cricket with Dad," said Sanaya. "Had to prove I could field better than the boys." Imitating an almost side-on throw of a pro-cricketer.

"He'd be proud of your water balloon technique."

She nodded, sat on her hands, leaning forward on the metal bench.

The tranquil Yarra River in front of them balanced the thumping bass beat echoing behind them from the festival party. Which mirrored his inner world; he'd slotted into Sanaya's unexpected appearance like they'd never broken up, as his heart beat a little faster, louder. Although it wasn't totally unexpected. While focusing on his video gig, the prospect that Sanaya may have been at the festival made him second-glance at a dozen women with long black hair.

"That's amazing work you're doing with Andy and Simon at Portable. You've really found your niche."

"Thanks," she said to the Yarra.

"Did being with an old dude like me inspire your games for dementia?"

Sanaya didn't laugh. She stiffened up and turned to him, a darkness across her face he'd never seen.

"Dad has dementia. Had to stop working."

"Oh, Sanaya." He opened his arms and she leaned in for his hug.

He thought he was comforting her, but it wasn't sympathy, which was often disguised as love, a joyous symphony sang to his soul. No matter what plans their brains had laid out, their hearts orchestrated a different melody.

"At least Mom has something to focus on now instead of calling me about boys every second day." She shifted and rested her head on his shoulder, an arm around his waist.

He squeezed her shoulder.

"You've done okay for an old dude, too. That story you filmed with that man talking about putting a gun under his chin, but not giving up, then having a kick of the soccer ball with his son, made me cry."

"Thanks, he was brave repeating that stuff on camera. So you follow all my work?"

"Ego-man hasn't changed a bit."

"Something's changed." He straightened up and eased Sanaya to face him. Held her hands. "I understand if you don't trust me after… but I miss you. Your boombox laugh, your cheeky digs at me, the way you pick at threads on clothes or other fabric. I don't want to miss another moment I can share with you."

He could hear the cox shouting to a rowing crew as they glided past on the Yarra, but he dared not take his eyes off Sanaya. Desperate to read any signal. Any emotion. She stared at him for eons. Blank stare.

"You hurt me. It was like pain held a global convention, all the pain in the world came together and my stomach, head and heart were the venues."

"I'm sorry Sanaya, so sorry."

"I've forgiven you."

He kissed her hands gently three times.

"I trust you Leo, but…I can't trust a future together."

"I get—"

She raised her hands as stop signs.

"Being together and being apart has helped me realize I do want to be a mom. I want to have one child. Not today, not tomorrow, but someday. And it's obvious our algorithms aren't aligned. And I get it, I don't take it as a personal rejection. You've worked hard to be a good dad and now you have other goals. That's your life-game logic, not mine. If we stayed together it would've been as sad as a Holi festival without color."

Her posture was comfortable, upright, but not tense. Hands resting one on the other on her thigh. Eyes soft, stunning.

"The Holi Festival is all about forgiveness, new starts; it brought us together so we can say goodbye to our relationship with love, not pain." She pointed at his white shirt, now splattered with color. "Closure with happy colors."

Sanaya may have been conducting a final sonata, but his heart was still reveling in a romantic symphony.

"Something I never told you… my vasectomy is reversible."

⁂

Sanaya's brain hardware registered the words.

My vasectomy is reversible.

She grasped the coding, the basic logic of Leo's statement, yet it crashed her system. She'd worked hard to reprogram her heart, her life algorithms, but not for that move.

My vasectomy is reversible.

Is he joking? Is it a desperate ploy to seduce her?

She scanned his left eye, right eye; love and his sparkle of life bored back at her. Deep in her soul an uncontrollable urge, like an artificial intelligence, pushed her to hug him. It wasn't strong enough to hold down the fear in her gut and heart.

"You never mentioned it before. Why now?" she said.

"We never really had the conversation."

"Because you dumped me cold turkey."

Leo edged closer. She bounced up, crossed the path, focused on the river. The sun had disappeared to their right, a party boat lit in colored lights floated past; music competing with loud boys, and women in shimmering dresses.

Leo, stepped over the little concrete wall and stood on the grass embankment facing her. The slight hill put them at eye level.

"I love you, Sanaya, and would have a baby with you. Only you. I'm willing to redesign my whole future for you."

"What if the reversal doesn't work?"

"My vasectomy was performed by Professor Earl Owen, he invented the procedure. It was just a fluke I was referred to him when I was living in Sydney, but it's true."

"What…what if it's too late?"

"We'll adopt," he said. "If that's what you want."

All she wanted eighteen months ago stood in front of her now. In recent months, she'd definitely wanted more. Her own child. Boy or girl. To raise with someone she loved and trusted. Non-negotiable. Leo wasn't part of that vision.

"All I ask is that we spend a year living together first, to make sure we both feel the same way after four seasons, then we make it forever."

"All these words so we have sex sooner?"

"No, every word is from my heart, the decision to have a child from deep in my soul."

Leo's sincerity so intense she had to turn away. She never goes out to meet someone but was open to the possibility. Connecting with someone at the Holi festival would have established one immediate level of compatibility, a solid start. Suddenly, nothing was solid. She was standing still but everything was spinning. She wanted Leo, wanted a baby, and now could have both.

"So you're ok with no sex till marriage?" She had no idea how the attack slipped out of her mouth, could almost taste the venom.

Leo didn't blink. He smiled. "At our age, with our feelings, why deprive ourselves of the beautiful, spiritual joy of making love?"

She couldn't fight his words, her body already melting under his gaze.

She ran.

Ran across the path, across the grass; zig-zagged through the crowd on the hill near the festival party and kept going till she was buried deep in the forest of gyrating bodies.

❃ 19 ❃

FESTIVAL OF LOVE

Sanaya danced like Lakshmi was watching.

No one else existed. The modern Indian beat wasn't her favorite but her body melded to the music. Boys stared, boys tried talking, but she only flirted with the music. Camouflaged in the hub of thousands, Leo had no hope of finding her. He'd probably gone home. She needed time to sort through what he'd said and why she'd fled. Surrounded by joy and everyone splattered in glorious color, her inner world grey.

Was she afraid of being dumped again? Wasn't that danger a possibility with any new guy? Isn't she one step closer to safety with Leo after what they've been through? His baby decision was a giant step. Galaxy crossing step. So why did she run? She'd pined for Leo through torturous pain. She wanted a baby. Leo had popped up at the Festival and presented both on a platter. Why the fear?

The music stopped. A few people pointed at the giant screen next to the stage.

'Sanaya G. This is for you, from Leo.' Filled the screen.

Her favorite Bollywood song from 'Rock On' blared out of the speakers and the crowd erupted in cheers and dance. Yet they all kept facing the stage. She inched around to get a glimpse amongst the bopping heads.

Leo.

On stage dancing like a dag.

To the song her troupe had performed nearly two years ago.

Leo gave it more energy and antics than that night in Collingwood. The DJ joined him and she gyrated like a pro. Leo tried to follow her moves and everyone laughed. Leo might've been the oldest dude in the huge joint but he was also more comfortable in his own skin and freer in his dancing. The DJ shimmied back to her console and the screen beamed one giant word:

SANAYA

Her name flashed slowly on and off. The crowd chanted her name every time it appeared.

"Sanaya… Sanaya…Sanaya…"

She found herself drifting towards the side of the stage. A security guard stopped her at the steps. She pointed at the screen and yelled above the music that she was Sanaya and the guy let her through.

The DJ saw her, gave her a double thumbs up then fiddled with the console. Her name flashed on the screen, bigger than a house, quicker and quicker.

"Sanaya, Sanaya, Sanaya…" chanted the crowd.

Leo came out of his dance trance and broke out a smile. He melted every molecule in her simmering body.

She danced towards him and the crowd erupted, cheering, whistling.

"Sanaya, Sanaya, Sanaya…" louder, faster.

Leo responded to her dancing, trying so hard now he was all over the place except on beat. She couldn't imagine loving Leo more than the way she loved him in that moment. Heat and joy poured out of her heart and ravaged her entire body.

She stopped dancing.

He stopped.

"Two years," she yelled.

"Two?"

She stepped closer. "One year dating, then we live together for one. If we're still talking, we can start our little family."

Leo's smile made the stage lights jealous. He picked her up and swung her around and around and around.

The crowd found another thousand decibels in cheers and whistles.

Leo let her slide down and held her tight. Which was just as well because she was dizzy from head to heart, tummy to toes.

"I love you," he said.

"I love you." The surest thing she'd ever said in her life. A feeling so solid she could build the Taj Mahal on it.

"But I don't think I can last one more year without spoiling you." His grin and sizzling eyes made it clear what 'spoiling' meant.

She'd been fantasizing about his solar hands even before he'd ended their relationship. No way she was going to last a year either.

"Maybe we can start with a massage soon. After one of my dance classes."

Wide sizzling eyes, goofy giant grin.

She kissed him.

The crowd went wild

She kissed like a Lakshmi, but instead of four hands she had four searing tongues; searching, tasting, teasing, devouring.

And Leo devoured right back.

When she pulled back to confirm it was all really happening, Leo kissed his palm and placed it on her heart. She kissed her palm and placed it on his heart. Kisses for their scars. Dr Tatarka had taught her that wounds heal from the inside. Physical wounds, emotional wounds. Sanaya discovered the secret medicine was love and kindness to yourself. She'd accepted her scars, took responsibility for healing. She was ready to pour her love onto Leo and bathe in his. She'd kissed her scars and now all she wanted was to kiss Leo.

Every day. Forever.

Writers sweat blood to get stories out into the world and reviews are our super-food.
Every time you leave a kind review, you're doing a wonderful deed for all writers, all stories. Thanks, Jim.

Don't miss Jim's debut novel, *Up Here*

When you've had two dream marriages, choosing your eternal soulmate in heaven is one hell of a dilemma.

www.JimShomos.com/up-here

The most original romantic-comedy this century. Artisan Book Reviews, 5*

Up Here touched my soul, a beautiful romantic comedy about love, hope and courage. Alli, 5*

Jim Shomos must have written this with a twinkle in his eyes, as moving, as it is funny. Ella, 5*

Get VIP release news about Jim's coming books at:
www.JimShomos.com

ACKNOWLEDGMENTS

To Sunface, 'Sanaya'. Our story ended at the Goodbye Café scene but I hope this book reflects the crazy-zany, creativity and kindness of our time together. At the request of 'Sanaya', her original poems were replaced. All of the poems attributed to 'Sanaya' are written by me.

The Romance Writer's Australia, I've only attended 1 ½ conferences, yet met some generous and talented writers I can always turn to in times of panic: Lauren, Michelle, Effie and Alli contributed to elements of Kissing Scars.

To the four foundation pillars of friendship that support my writing, while slapping my ego with the humor it deserves: Bruce, Paul, Chris, and Ted. Mary C, for your invaluable input again. Bridget B, for slogging through a horrible first draft of this story long ago without un-friending me.

Shannon, you are a dream editor and I look forward to collaborating on our next book. Jo for designing one of the most stunning fiction book covers of 2021. Megumi, you still haven't thrown me out, our love story continues...

Life can drown in details
It's a slow torture without love
My scars are my guiding map Wherever
you go, I'll find you

Love, courage and destiny
Are my three Musketeers
One for all and all for you
Whatever it takes, I'll find you

Beggars can dance
The blind can sing
From slums to millionaires
Sinners and desperate prayers
Only love can bring
Kisses for our scars

Life can pass you by
While you're waiting for the wrong train
There's no schedule for love
Look into my eyes, you know me

Ask me any question
They all lead to the same answer
You don't need someone's nod
Time to trust your heart, you know me

Beggars can dance

The blind can sing
From slums to millionaires
Sinners and desperate prayers
Only love can bring
Kisses for our scars

JIM SHOMOS

Over 22 years Jim's stories have skipped across film, TV, web, songs and novels. An international pioneer in web series, he has collected nominations and awards in Cannes, Film Victoria and from the Australian Writers' Guild.

"I'm a ro-man-tic, hooked on exploring contemporary relationships through fiction. Sprinkling love, laughter and sneaky tears."

Rumors of an insatiable passion for Haigh's Chocolates, Arsenal, Melbourne Victory cycling and blueberry muffins. Sometimes cycling for blueberry muffins.

Jim's first novel published in 2020, Up Here, began life as a screenplay and was shortlisted in Top-5 of the Australian Writers' Guild 'Romantic-comedy competition' alongside The Rosie Project.

When you've had two dream marriages, choosing your eternal soulmate in heaven is one hell of a dilemma.

www.JimShomos.com/up-here

A one-of-a-kind romantic-comedy that shouldn't work but masterfully does. Never Ending Bookshelf.

I love this quirky story. What a tricky situation Peter is in! This will have you giggling. Blaise, 5*

Wonderful romantic comedy. By far the best book I have read this year. Jewel, 5* (September 2020).

I loved this romantic comedy. It is so heart-warming, funny and relatable. Ellery, 5*

Get VIP release news by subscribing to his newsletter at:
www.JimShomos.com

www.ingramcontent.com/pod-product-compliance
Lightning Source LLC
Chambersburg PA
CBHW020640130726
47903CB00003BA/931

* 9 7 8 0 6 4 5 0 4 5 8 1 9 *